THE GOOD PILOT
PETER WOODHOUSE

ALEXANDER McCALL SMITH

THE GOOD PILOT PETER WOODHOUSE

A Wartime Romance

Polygon

First published in Great Britain in 2017 by
Polygon, an imprint of Birlinn Ltd
West Newington House
10 Newington Road
Edinburgh
EH9 1QS

www.polygonbooks.co.uk

ISBN 978 1 84697 409 0

British Library Cataloguing-in-Publication Data
A catalogue record for this book is available on request from the British Library

Typeset by Studio Monachino
Printed and bound by Clays Ltd, St Ives plc

THIS BOOK IS FOR
Michael and Angela Clarke

ONE

TINNED PEACHES

The farmer taught her to avoid blisters by spitting on her hands.

He looked at her in that sideways manner of his, and she noticed that his nose had veins just visible under the skin, forked and meandering, like tiny rivulets marked on a map. She knew that she should not stare at his nose; she had been taught by her aunt that she should never pay attention to any obvious physical feature. *People come in different shapes and sizes,* Annie said. *Don't make it awkward for them.*

She wrested her gaze away from the farmer's nose and looked into his eyes, wondering what age he was. She was nineteen – twenty in a couple of months – and it was still difficult for her to judge the age of those even a decade older than she was. He was in his late fifties somewhere, she thought. His eyes, she noticed, were grey, and clear too; they were those of one who was used to the open, to wind and weather, to open spaces. They were a countryman's eyes, accustomed to looking at things that were really important: sheep, cattle, the ploughed earth – things that a farmer saw, and understood. She spotted these things; she may not have had much formal education – she had left school at sixteen, as many did – but she saw things that other people failed to see, and she understood them. They said at school that she could have gone much further, as she was of above average intelligence – a "thoughtful, articulate girl", the principal had written; "the sort of talent this country wastes so carelessly". University, even, had been a possibility, but there had not been much money and she had found the thought of going away was daunting.

"Spit on your hands, Val," he said. "Like this, see."

He spat on his right hand first, then the left. "Then you rub them together," he continued. "Not too much, mind, or it won't work. You try now. You show me."

She smiled, and looked down at her hands. They were already dirty from salvaging hessian sacks in one of the barns to stack them ready for use – nothing was wasted these days, old string, rusty nails, scraps of wood – everything could be put to some use. Her hands were still soft, though, and he had noticed.

"You don't mind if I call you Val?" asked the farmer. "It would be a bit of a mouthful to call you Miss . . ." He trailed away, looking momentarily embarrassed.

"Eliot. Miss Eliot. No, Val is who I am."

"And you should call me Archie. Full name Archibald, of course, but nobody ever used that – apart from my mother. Mothers usually call their sons by their proper names. I knew a lad at school who was called Skinny by everybody – he was that thin – but his mother always called him Terence." He shook his head at the memory. "Not much of a name, Terence, if you ask me. A town name, I'd say."

She laughed. "My aunt sometimes calls me Valerie. Same thing, I suppose." She paused. "So I should spit on my hands when I'm picking things?"

"Yes, if you like. But mostly when you're using a spade. The handle can be hard on your hands. I've seen young lads get blisters the size of a half-crown from spades."

She promised to be careful, and to remember to do as he said. There was so much to learn: she been on the farm for only three days, and she had already learned eighteen things.

She had written them all down in her land girl's diary, each one numbered, with its explanation written in pencil. Eighteen new pieces of information as to how to work the land; about how to be a farmer.

They had been standing in the yard, directly outside the larger of the two barns. Now the farmer suggested that if she came to the farmhouse kitchen he would make tea for both of them. She should take a break every four hours, he said. "Take fifteen minutes to get your breath back. It's more efficient that way – at least in the long run. A tired man . . . sorry, a tired girl too . . . gets less done than one who's well rested. I've always said that. I told young Phil that. He was a one for working all hours, but I told him not to."

He had mentioned Phil on the first day. He had explained that he was his nephew, the son of his older brother, who had helped him on the farm for almost a year, and had gone off to join the army two months earlier. "He saw through Hitler," he said. "Even when he was a nipper, fourteen, fifteen, he said 'Hitler's trouble'. And he was right, wasn't he? Spot on. Look where we are now. Hitler sitting in all those countries – France, Holland, them places – and if it hadn't been for the Yanks coming in we'd be on our knees, begging for mercy."

He had welcomed her, because with Phil gone he would not have been able to cope. The farm was not a large one – eighty-five acres – but it was intensively cultivated and it would have been too much for him to manage by himself. That was where the Women's Land Army came in: they said they would send him one of their land girls, and they sent her, riding on her bicycle from the village six miles away. She lived there with her aunt Annie, the local postmistress. Archie knew Annie slightly, as the local postmistress was friendly with everybody. He must have seen Val about the place too, but had not noticed her. He did not pay much attention to women and girls; he was a shy man, who had never married, and tended to feel awkward in female company. But he liked Val; on that very first day he had decided that here was a well brought up girl who knew her manners and was not going to be afraid of hard work. She would earn her two pounds four shillings a week, he thought. It was a decent wage if you did not have to give up some of it for board and lodging – and he assumed she did not have to pay Annie for lodging, although she probably contributed something for her food. She might even be able to save – if she stayed the course, which he had a feeling she would do. If they had sent him somebody from town, it could be a very different story. He knew somebody who had been allocated a land girl from London and she barely knew that milk came from cows; there was no work in her, he had been told, just complaints about mud and requests for time off every other day. He would not have a girl like that about the place; he would refuse, and they couldn't make him take her, even with their powers to tell you to do this and that, as if the Ministry of Agriculture knew how to run a farm.

"So, Val Eliot," he said as he poured her mug of tea. "Tell me a little more about yourself. Where are your mum and dad?" He immediately regretted the question. He should not have asked her that, and he became flustered.

He was relieved that she did not seem upset. "My dad went to Australia," she said. "That was twelve years ago, when I was seven. My mum died five years ago."

Well, at least she was not an orphan; that would have made

his question all the more tactless. "I'm sorry about your mum," he said.

"My aunt is her sister," said Val. "She took me in. My dad sends money, sometimes, or did until last year, when I turned eighteen. But my aunt was all right with that. She says that my dad isn't a bad man; he's just not the sort to settle down. He moved around in Australia. He's a roofer. They have a lot of tin roofs out there." She paused. "You want to see a photograph of them? Of my mum and dad?"

He nodded, and she crossed the kitchen to the peg where he had told her she could hang the jacket and scarf she wore when cycling from the village. She took out a purse, and extracted from it a small photograph. The photograph had been posted onto card for protection.

"That's them," she said. "Before he left for Australia."

He looked at the picture of the man and woman standing outside a shop front. They were holding hands, dressed in their Sunday best, the man with one of those stiff, uncomfortable collars, the woman with a blouse that buttoned up to her neck.

"She has a kind face," he said. "I like her smile."

"My aunt says that my mum always smiled. All the time. She said that even when she felt low about something, she still smiled."

"That's the attitude," said Archie. "No use being down in the dumps. That never makes anything any easier."

"I think that too," she said.

Archie looked at her with admiration. If he had ever had a daughter, she would be something like this girl, he thought. That fellow who went off to Australia – he didn't deserve a daughter like this.

She was still working at six, when Archie told her she could stop.

"You should be getting home now," he said. "Lots of light still, but you'll be needing your tea."

She stood up, brushing the earth from her fingers. She had been weeding a line of cabbages and her knees and her back were sore from the bending.

"I don't have a watch," she said. "It broke."

He smiled. "No need for watches on a farm. There's the sun. It comes up and you know that's morning. Goes down and you know it's night. Simple, really."

He walked back with her towards the farmhouse. While she collected her scarf and coat, he made his way into a shed and emerged with a basket.

"I've got three eggs here for you," he said. "Fresh today. The hens are laying well. I think they like you."

She had fed the hens that morning and they had pecked and fluttered about her feet, desperate for the grain; silly creatures, she thought, with their fussing and clucking about nothing very much. Now she peered into the basket; he had wrapped each egg in a twist of newspaper, but she could see they were of a generous size. The ration was one egg a week for each person, and here were three.

"You're very kind," she said, taking the basket. "I'll bring the basket back tomorrow."

He nodded. "You say hello to your aunt from me."

"I shall."

"And ride carefully down that lane. Those trucks from the base sometimes come this way and they don't know how to drive, half of them."

"I'll be careful."

It took her forty minutes to reach the village. There were no cars – not a single one – and no trucks. This was deep England, far away from any big town, a self-contained world of secret, hedge-marked fields and short distances. Wheeling her bicycle into the back yard, she leaned it against the wall of the shed. Then she went inside, the eggs her trophy, proudly held before her.

Annie kissed her. "Clever girl," she said. "You must be working hard for him to treat you to those."

"He's a kind man, Auntie."

Annie agreed. "Everyone speaks highly of Archie Wilkinson." She began to unwrap the eggs. "They say he wanted to get married but never did. Too much work to do. Never got away from that farm of his." She paused. "It could still happen, of course. But look at these eggs: lovely brown shells. Look."

Val examined one of the eggs. "Made so perfectly, aren't they? So smooth."

"One each," said Annie. "Coddled? A coddled egg is hard to beat."

Val nodded. "Is Willy in yet?"

Willy was a relative – a distant connection by marriage – who had been staying with Annie for the last year. He was working on the land, too, although the farm to which he had been sent, a farm that belonged to a man called Ted Butters, was further away, and by all accounts very different from Archie's place. Not that they heard much about it from Willy, who was not very bright and forgot things easily. He was two years older than Val and had never been able to have a proper job. He had come to live with Annie when he had been sent to work on the farm, which was more or less all he could do.

"There's no danger of the army coming for Willy," Annie had observed. "Poor boy, but at least he's not going to have to put on a uniform. He'd never cope with army life."

Val got on well with Willy – it would be hard not to. She liked his openness, and his innocent, generous smile. "He's very gentle," she said to a friend who enquired about the rather ungainly young man she had seen coming out of the post office. "Willy wouldn't hurt a fly. But there's not much he can do really. He can pick potatoes and things like that, and precious little else."

Now Annie said, "Willy will like this egg. He loves eggs, doesn't he? I bet that farmer up there will not be giving him much. Mean piece of work."

Half an hour later they sat down at the kitchen table. Annie served the coddled eggs with pieces of bread on which she had scraped a thin layer of dripping.

"This is a real feast," said Val.

Willy beamed with pleasure. "I like eggs," he said. "Always have."

Val washed up, with the wireless on in the background. She listened to the announcer with his grave, clipped voice. Bad news given in measured tones could even sound reassuring. Willy, of course, only half grasped what was happening. "The desert's very dry," he remarked. "Where do they get the water for the tanks?"

"Oases," said Annie. It suddenly occurred to her that he might be thinking of water tanks, rather than armoured tanks. "But don't you worry about that, Willy."

"That's where camels go," he said. "That's so, isn't it? Them oases have wells and palm trees that give you those things, those nuts."

"Dates," said Val.

"The Americans are here, anyway," said Willy. "I saw some. Big fellows. They had one of those jeeps."

Val gazed out of the window. She did not mind the fact that her life was like this, with not very much going on; with Willy saying these odd, unconnected things, and her aunt with her knitting; but sometimes you wondered – you could not help yourself – you wondered whether it would be like this forever.

Ted Butters' farm, where Willy was now working, was large enough to be quite profitable, but was badly run. Ted was a mean-spirited man, and lazy too. A glance at a farmer's fields will tell you all you need to know about his character: a well-kept farm, with fences in good order and well-cared-for livestock, is a sign of a hard-working farmer who understands the notion of stewardship. Badly drained fields, rank grazing land on which weeds have gained the upper hand, a farmyard littered with malfunctioning machinery; these all betray the presence of a farmer who has given up, or who drinks, or who simply does not know what he is doing. People knew what Ted Butters was like, and it was only a matter of time, some thought, before he was dealt with by the local War Agricultural Executive Committee. It would sort him out, they said; it would put him off the land and let somebody else take over.

The committees had been given wide powers. They could order unproductive land to be ploughed up; they could tell farmers what crops to grow; and, if defied or disobeyed, they could order the offender to quit his farm. Such powers were justified by the emergency of the moment: the country needed food, and every square inch of ground would have to be used – and used well – if the land were to yield crops to its capacity. Nobody could argue with that.

Ted Butters was exactly the sort of farmer who might be expected to fall foul of the local War Ag committee. And he would have done so, were it not for the fact that in spite of his sloppiness and the dereliction of his land, he managed –

against all the odds – to produce good harvests. And perhaps even more important, there was something between him and the chairman of the committee. The chairman would listen to rumblings about Ted but would never comment on what he heard. Nor would he act. "Ted has something over him," people whispered. "He owes Ted money, I shouldn't wonder."

"Unfair, isn't it? Others get booted out of their farms and Ted gets away with it."

"One of these days they'll catch up with him, so they will."

"Don't hold your breath."

The worst consequence of Ted Butters' negligence was the state of his livestock. His farm was mostly arable land, but he kept a few animals because his father had always kept them and Ted could not be bothered to do anything differently from his father. These animals included two cows, a flock of just under thirty sheep, and two dogs.

"You any good with animals?" Ted asked Willy when he first arrived, brought to the farm by a Ministry of Agriculture official. The official remained silent; he was watching. He had not thought that Willy would be up to this job, but he had been overruled.

Willy nodded enthusiastically. "God loves them," he said.

Ted looked at him. "Cows? You know how to milk a cow?"

Again, Willy nodded. "You pull . . . you pull those things. The milk comes out. It goes into the bucket."

"Bright lad this," whispered the official.

Ted had accepted him grudgingly, but he had his suspicions. "You'd think they'd send me a couple of those girls," he remarked. "Those land girls. Do they send them my way? None of it. I get the dolt. Maybe he's somebody's eyes and ears – who knows?"

Willy was keen. He was taught to milk the cows and gradually mastered the technique. He was good at muck-spreading – pitching the manure from the cart over the fields, spreading it with his fork, indifferent to the stench.

"That stuff's good for plants," he said to Annie. "They grow like crazy."

"I can imagine it, Willy," said Annie. "You're learning so much, aren't you?"

"Could be," said Willy.

Willy was in charge of bringing the cows in for milking but did not have much to do with the sheep because the sheepdog would not listen to him if he tried to give commands.

"The dog senses that he doesn't know what he's doing," confided the farmer when the committee came to inspect the farm.

"You're doing a good deed, keeping that boy," said the chairman.

Ted shrugged. He had regarded Willy as a nuisance, but now he was satisfied that the young man was harmless – and was useful enough, in his way. "He doesn't seem to know very much," he said. "But he knows how to pull weeds and he's handy enough with a bale of hay. Can't complain, I suppose, though some places have got three, even four, land girls. Why not me? The government think there's something wrong with me?"

Willy noticed things. For all that his conversation followed its own idiosyncratic path, for all that he would turn away in the middle of an exchange and start doing something else, he could see what was going on. He noticed the occasional visits of the two men who drove up to the farm in a small green van, loaded boxes, and then drove away again without going into the farmhouse. He knew that the boxes contained chickens that Ted had slaughtered in one of the barns amidst great squawking and clouds of feathers. He knew that meat was precious and that you could not buy chickens off the ration. But the farmer had said to him, right at the beginning, "Anything you see around here, my boy, you keep to yourself, understand? No poking your nose into things that don't concern you." And had accompanied this with a gesture that Willy correctly interpreted as somehow threatening him, a ringing motion, as if he were strangling a chicken.

Ted need not have worried about Willy's reporting anything of that; the young man was not interested in such matters. But what did interest him was the condition of the animals, even if he had no idea that anything could be done about it. He noticed that the cows were lame; somebody had explained to him that hooves needed to be trimmed and if this were not done regularly, could be painful for the animal. He pointed this out to Ted, who was indifferent. "They can walk, can't they? Nothing wrong with those cows."

Willy was responsible for the feeding of the two sheepdogs, Border collies, who were housed in a small shed at the back of the barn. These dogs were mother and son, Willy having put the mother to a dog owned by another farmer down in Somerset. He had done so to sell the puppies, of which there were four; good prices would be paid for a good-looking sheepdog, and he disposed of three of them within a few hours at the local market. He kept the fourth, because the mother was getting on and he would need a dog to train up to take her place.

Willy wondered why the dogs got no meat, but were given a plain porridge topped up with a few unidentifiable kitchen scraps. It was the sort of food one gave to pigs, he thought, rather than dogs. Why not give the dogs rabbit? There were enough of those on the farm and Ted could easily shoot a few for the dogs' pot. It was unkind, he thought, to deny a dog meat and to keep it tethered for days on end, as Ted did, in that darkened shed.

The dogs liked Willy and whimpered as he bent down to stroke them.

"You poor fellows," he said, allowing them to lick him on the arms, on the face. "Someday things will get better for you. When the war's over, maybe. Maybe then."

He watched Ted as he tried to train the younger dog. He used a stick, a branch he cut from the patch of willows near his pond, and he wielded this with a vicious determination. He beat the mother dog too, who cowered when he approached, scraping the ground with her belly, rolling over in the classic canine pose of submission, her legs cycling in the air as if to defend herself from impending blows.

"Bite him, bite him," muttered Willy under his breath.

He told Annie about this. "Ted Butters beats the dogs," he said.

She raised an eyebrow. "Oh yes? When they do something wrong?"

Willy shook his head. "Just for being dogs. He beats them because they're dogs."

Annie looked at him. He had an odd turn of phrase, that boy, she thought; sometimes he said things that made you stop and think. "For no reason?" She shook her head. "He's not a very nice man, that Ted Butters. Never was."

"With a stick," said Willy.

Annie sighed. It was too small a wrong to make a fuss about, and nobody would interfere with the way a farmer treated his dogs. For most people, that was the farmer's business. "Lots of people are unkind to dogs, Willy." She paused. "He doesn't lay a finger on you, does he?" You had to be careful; Willy was not much more than a boy, really, and there were some men who had to be watched when it came to boys.

Willy looked at her blankly. "Me?"

"He doesn't beat you? Or anything?"

He laughed. "No, I said that he beats the dogs, not me. He beats them."

Val had overheard this conversation. She had been sitting in a corner of the kitchen with a magazine. There was very little to read, because of the paper shortages, but she had obtained this from a friend on the promise that she would give it back. It had pictures of the king and queen inspecting a house that had been bombed. They were not worried about bombs, said the report. They carried on with their duties in spite of everything that Hitler could throw at them.

She looked up. "I hate people who mistreat dogs," she said. "That man . . ."

"They should run away," said Willy. "Dogs can run away, I think."

Val turned a page of the magazine. 'Sometimes they do," she said.

Willy was watching her. He knew that Val would be kind to dogs. They would love her, those dogs at the farm; they would lick her just as they licked him. They would appreciate somebody like Val.

The new planes arrived one morning, all coming from the same direction, dropping down below the trees just before they landed, seeming to disappear into the countryside. But even after they disappeared they could be heard, their throaty growl rising up into the sky, before this eventually died away and silence ensued. She said to Archie, "One flew right over me. Like an eagle swooping down. Big thing. Almost knocked me off the bike."

"American planes," he said. "They never told us, but they're going to be staying at the base. They were cutting the grass on the airfield. I saw that going on and thought they might be expecting visitors. They're setting up their own base, right next to ours."

"All the way from America," said Val.

Archie nodded. "And a good thing too. Give Goering something to think about, I'm sure. Old Fatty with his blue uniform."

There were not many planes, and their flying patterns seemed erratic. A fighter base would have had constant comings and goings, but this sent out no more than a flight or two a day, aircraft that Archie identified as Mosquitoes, but in US Air Force livery.

"I know we're not meant to talk about it," he said to Val, "but I heard down at the pub that they're reconnaissance people. They fly off and take photographs of what Jerry's up to. Railway lines, factories – stuff like that."

She spoke in mock admonishment. "Careless talk costs . . ."

He stopped her. "I'm only saying what I heard."

"Well, we'll see."

She got on with her work, which that day was weeding a field of carrots. She used a hoe to begin with, but damaged so many of the carrot-tops that she laid it aside and began to do the task by hand. The field was not a big one, but ploughed and sown it had produced what seemed to Val to be a sea of carrot-tops. Archie had said she could take her time – that the task would normally have kept three or four people busy – but her slow progress was an affront to her own sense of urgency. It was as if the fate of air battles fought far away was somehow dependent on her ability to clear the carrot field of weeds; she thought of the weeds as enemies – each one plucked and tossed aside was another Nazi dealt with.

Her back started to trouble her and there were other muscles, too, that she was only just discovering. There was a crick in her neck that brought on a vague ache somewhere at the back of her head. She stood up and stretched, trying to loosen and unknot her aching muscles. She thought: *What if this war goes on indefinitely?* She had not learned much history at school, but she had heard of the Hundred Years War. If it had happened before, then surely it could happen again: her children, if she ever had any, could be weeding this carrot field for year after year before passing it on to their own children.

She mentioned this to Archie. "There was a hundred years war once, you know. A long time ago, but it lasted for a hundred years."

Archie set her mind at rest. "A hundred years? No, more like a hundred days. Jerry won't stand a chance now that the Americans are here. A hundred days should do it, I'm reckoning."

"But the Germans still . . ."

He did not let her finish. "They're no match," he said. "There are these American factories, see, turning out hundreds of planes a day. Hundreds. Rolling them out."

"I hope you're right."

An American serviceman came to the farm to ask about eggs. He arrived in a jeep, being driven too fast, with a younger man who remained at the wheel and did not get out. This younger man had an angry skin, pitted and red; he looked barely eighteen, and he avoided eye contact. He was one of those people, Val thought, who was probably always unhappy to be where he was. There were people like that. They were both dressed in uniform of some sort, or working clothes, perhaps, as it seemed very casual.

The older man said that he was from the base. "We're looking for more eggs," he said. "We get a lot of our rations centrally, but not enough eggs."

Archie scratched his head. "I could speak to the hens."

The man laughed. "Sure, speak to the hens. Any chance?"

Archie looked over in the direction of the hen coop. "I could get a few more chickens. If I did, I could do maybe four or five dozen a week. Depends on the hens, though."

"Every little helps," said the man. "Can you deliver to the base?"

"I can send the girl," said Archie.

Val glared at him, but then she smiled at the man. "I can bring them," she said. "On my bike."

The man smiled. "That's mighty helpful of you, m'am."

Val thought it was better to be *m'am* than *the girl*. She hoped that Archie noticed. Afterwards, when the jeep had gone, she remarked to Archie, "They have good manners, those Americans."

Archie nodded. "Yes, but they speak all peculiar."

"They probably think we do," said Val.

Archie looked surprised. "Us? No, we speak English as it's meant to be spoken. It's them that's got it wrong."

A week later she made the first delivery. The base was about eight miles away, and it took her a good hour to reach it on her bicycle, three dozen eggs safely stored in the handlebar basket. They had warned the sentries of her arrival and she was waved through after the eggs had been inspected.

"Nice," said the sentry, and added, "For the officers, I bet."

He directed her to an office, a Nissen hut with a large sign on its front. It was a scene of busyness: men were milling about; planes lined the edge of the runway; a mechanic stood on the wings of one and shouted to another man below.

A thin man in civilian clothes asked her what she wanted. She explained that the eggs were for Sergeant Lisowski; it was the name of the man who had come to the farm, and she stumbled over it. But the thin man knew who it was. "Cookhouse," he said. "I'll call him."

A figure emerged from the door. He was walking somewhere purposively, but stopped, and turned his head. He looked at Val.

"Something good in there?" he asked, gesturing to the basket.

She was shy. He was wearing uniform and there was something unusual about him. She glanced at his face. It was the eyes, which were blue, and the regularity of the features, perhaps, and the way he seemed to be smiling at her without really smiling.

"Eggs," she said. "Eggs from the farm. They're for Sergeant Lis . . ." Again she stumbled over the name.

He grinned. "Lisowski?"

"Yes."

Something made her want to prolong the conversation. She reached for one of the small cardboard boxes in which the eggs were stored. She took it out and prised open the lid. He peered into it, and as he did so, the box slipped out of her hand and fell to the ground.

He reached forward in an attempt to catch it as it fell, but he was too late. Hitting the ground with a dull thud, the box disgorged several of its eggs. Val gasped, and instinctively bent down to retrieve them, upsetting her bicycle as she did so. Slowly, but irretrievably, the bicycle toppled over, tipping out the remaining two boxes of eggs.

"Oh, no . . ."

She wanted to cry, and almost did. She felt flustered and embarrassed. They were all broken, she thought; every one of them. Eggshell lay on the ground covered with slippery, translucent white. Streaks of rich yellow yolk mixed with the viscous white and with grit on the ground below.

His face registered his dismay. "Oh my, this isn't so good."

She looked up at him – they were both crouched down in an attempt to fix the unfixable.

"Could be worse," he said, straightening up. "Eggs are just eggs, after all."

She started to pick up her fallen bicycle, but he was there

before her. "There," he said. "I'll get you something to wipe your hands."

"I don't need anything," she said, and then, lest she sound churlish, "Thank you anyway. I'm all right."

"Pity about the eggs," he said. "Do you want me to square it with Lisowski?"

She shook her head in her confusion.

"I guess I should introduce myself," he said. "My name's Mike."

"I'm Val."

He nodded, and then glanced at his watch. "You're from round here?"

She told him about the farm.

"I've probably flown right over your place," he said.

"Probably."

"I hope I didn't give you a fright."

She told him she was accustomed to planes.

He looked at his watch again. "I could give you a ride home," he said. "I come off duty in twenty minutes. I could take you – and your bike – back to the farm."

She wanted to spend more time with him; she did not want the acquaintance to end. She felt something unfamiliar in her stomach: a lightness. She looked down at the ground. "You don't mind?"

He shook his head. He was smiling now and she saw that there was a dimple in each cheek – perfectly placed. It was a boyish face, clean-cut, the features regular. There was an openness about it, too, that gave it a strong sense of innocence. She thought he was probably a bit older than she was – perhaps mid-twenties – but it was hard to tell. She had heard people say that Americans looked younger than British people; a friend had told her it was because of the food they ate – "buckets of ice cream and corn on the cob and such things."

He was telling her he did not mind. "It would be a pleasure. We can take a jeep – official, you see, on the grounds that we need to replace a few eggs. Your bike can go on the back."

Annie said to Willy, "Now, Willy, you're going to have to take your shirt off."

Willy looked resentful. "Don't like taking my clothes off. Not with women around."

"It's just your shirt, Willy. And if you think we haven't seen men's chests before, then you don't know very much about anything."

He hesitated, and then began to unbutton the shirt. Annie looked away in a gesture to his modesty.

"Turn around," she said.

Holding the shirt in front of him, he turned his back to her, and she gasped.

"That devil," she exclaimed.

"He only hit me once," said Willy.

She reached forward and put a finger on the weal. He gave a start.

"That hurts, doesn't it?"

"It's not bad. I told you: he only hit me once and I don't want any fuss."

She walked round to his front and took his hands in hers. "What with, Willy? What did he hit you with?"

"He had a sort of whip. Those fellows who walk with the hounds carry them. I've seen them."

She drew in her breath. "You can do a lot of damage with those things." She paused, and returned to her examination of the weal. "I don't think the skin's broken."

"I told you, it's not a big thing."

"Put your shirt back on. But I'm going to watch that – I'll look at it again tomorrow, and if needs be we'll get Nurse Simpson."

"I don't need to see her."

"I'll be the judge of that, Willy." Her manner had become stern. "Do as I say now."

He put his shirt back on, buttoning it right up to the collar.

"I'm not having him raising a hand to you," said Annie. "You're a grown lad, Willy – you're not . . . you're not some boy." She paused. "Why did he do it? What was it all about?"

Willy bit his lip. When he answered, his tone was reluctant. "He was beating one of the dogs."

She stared at him. "And you tried to stop him?"

It took him a while to answer, but finally he said, "They'd killed one of the chickens. Dogs do that. They don't know any better."

She frowned. "So what did you do, Willy?"

He sniffed. "I grabbed the whip from him. I hit him with it – I wanted him to see what it felt like. Even if you're a dog . . ."

She stopped him. "You mean you struck him first?"

He stared at the ground. "Maybe. But he was beating the dog and she had done nothing to deserve it."

"Other than killing a chicken . . ."

He pouted. "It's in their nature. I said, that's what dogs do."

She nodded. "You're right. And you shouldn't beat an animal – it's not right."

"No, it isn't."

She reached out for his hand, and held it gently in hers. "The problem is, Willy, that you started this fight, you know. You struck him, and he'll just say that he was defending himself.

You know how these things work, don't you?" She suspected he did not.

He looked confused.

"If you hit somebody, he can hit you back?"

Annie sighed. "I think we should leave it, Willy. I was going to go to Bill Edwards about this . . ." Bill Edwards was the village policeman, brought back out of retirement because of the war; too tired to exert authority, he relied on friendship to police his patch. "But now I think I shouldn't."

"No, you shouldn't. I told you I didn't want any fuss."

"But you promise me that you won't provoke that man again. You promise me that?"

He crossed his heart – a childish gesture – but one that signalled to her that he had understood.

"Good boy," she said.

Later that night, when Willy had gone to bed, Annie talked to Val about what had happened. She expressed the concern that the young man's lack of judgement could cause difficulties. "Any sensible person would have known not to interfere in something like that," she said. "Farmers and their dogs – you stay out of it, even if it's hard to do. And a man like Ted Butters . . ." She shook her head. "You don't go laying into him."

Val felt she had to smile. "I don't suppose you do."

"Willy has a strong sense of right and wrong," Annie continued.

"Even if he hasn't much sense about anything else," said Val.

Annie looked disapproving. "He does his best," she said.

Val decided to change the subject. "I'm going out tomorrow night," she said.

"With the other land girls?' There was a group of five land girls billeted in a big house on the edge of the village.

"Yes," said Val. "We've been invited to a dance."

Annie took up her knitting. She had been working on a sweater for weeks and was frustrated at not finishing it. "Very nice. RAF?"

"The Americans," said Val.

Annie smiled. "They say they have tinned peaches. Have you heard that too?"

Val had not. "Nylons, some say. And chocolate."

"I don't think men should give girls nylons," said Annie. "Chocolate is one thing, but nylons . . ."

"If I see any tinned peaches," Val promised, "I'll bring some back for you."

Annie laid down her knitting and closed her eyes. There was a look on her face that was half longing, half ecstasy. "Just imagine – a bowl of tinned peaches with a drop of cream. Just imagine it."

"You never know," said Val.

Annie opened her eyes. "Don't be too late. Will they be bringing you back home with the others?"

"They will," said Val. "They have a lorry. It's ever so bumpy, travelling in the back of it, but they'll bring us right to the door."

It was not a large dance. She, like the others, had been to larger ones at an RAF base twenty miles away, but what made the difference here was the catering. The US Air Force may have been looking around for extra supplies of fresh eggs, but there was no shortage of anything else. Two trestle tables,

laid with red gingham tablecloths, were laid out with things
that had long since disappeared from the shelves of British
groceries, or had never been there in the first place. And
there were tinned peaches, but in bowls now, and she could
not think of a way to get some back to her aunt. She could
wrap one in a handkerchief, perhaps, but without its syrup it
would not be the same, and it would stain her dress anyway.
So she thought of her aunt as she helped herself to three peach
halves, savouring their sheer deliciousness and wondering
how one might describe the taste and the sensation accurately.
There was the sweetness, of course, but there was something
else – a slight roughness on the tongue that gave them their
characteristic texture. Or perhaps she should not mention
them at all, but simply say that the food was good, and leave
her aunt to imagine the rest.

She looked out for Mike, who had driven her home after the
egg incident, but although there were only twenty or so officers
there she did not see him. She felt a pang of disappointment:
she had assumed that he had been behind her invitation,
and now she was not sure. Perhaps she had been too quick
to imagine that there was something there when there really
was not. Perhaps she was just another young woman to him,
nothing more than that – the girl who rode over with the eggs
and clumsily dropped them all over the place. Perhaps he felt
sorry for her. Americans were rich – they had so much – and
the British were so poor now, scrabbling around for enough
food to eat, counting every round of ammunition, every drop
of fuel. She thought: *What do we look like to them?* Poor cousins
who were exhausted by a long fight against the local bully and
must now be helped to finish something they could never have

completed by themselves.

After the guests had been there for ten minutes, he arrived with another two officers. He was in uniform, as a few of the men were, the others being in civilian clothes. He made straight for her, and briefly took her hand, in what could have been a handshake or could have been something else. He held it, though, and only dropped it when he went to get a drink for both of them, and as she watched him cross the floor towards the bar she thought, with pleasure, that she had been right – he had invited her. It was him.

They had organised a small band – two saxophones, a trombone, and a percussionist. This quartet now struck up, although people were still helping themselves to plates of food and were not ready to dance. She sat with him on a small sofa that had been put along the side of the room and sipped at her drink, conscious that her dress, of which she had been proud until then, was almost dowdy by comparison with what some of the other women had managed to produce.

But he said, "I like that," and gestured to the dress. "It's pretty."

She lowered her eyes. She was not sure whether she should say that she liked his uniform. There were so many bewildering uniforms now and a compliment directed at a uniform could seem flat, or even sarcastic.

She struggled to think of something to say and ended up asking where he was from.

"The United States of America," he replied, and laughed.

This helped. "Oh, I know that."

His eyes were bright, as if he were amused by something. "Just making sure."

"But where in America? It's a big place, isn't it?"

"A place called Muncie, Indiana. It's not right in the middle, but it's heading that way. Mid-West, we call it. You heard of Chicago?"

She gave him a look of mock reproach. "Of course I've heard of Chicago." She was trying to think where Chicago was. Was it near Los Angeles?

"Well, Muncie, Indiana isn't all that far from Chicago – a few hundred miles. Chicago's there . . ." he jabbed at a point in the air, "and Muncie's down here." He made another jab.

"I see."

"It's not a very big town," he continued. "But we've got some great things going on. You know those glass jars for preserving fruit? You know them?"

She nodded, although she thought the glass jars he was referring to must be much bigger and better than the ones her aunt used for making jam in the blackberry season.

"We make those in Muncie," he said. "Invented there. Those famous jars. There's the Ball glassworks. You heard of them over here – the Ball family?"

She had not.

"They're generous folks," he continued. "They helped build a college, and a hospital. My mother knew one of the sisters from that family – not very well, but she knew her. She lived in a big mansion near the river, and you know what? She believed in fairies. She was real keen on fairies. She had a whole library of books about them and pictures on the wall and so on. Fairies flying around, sitting on bushes, doing everything really. I guess she was hoping to see one herself some time, but she never did, poor lady."

She was wide-eyed. This was a world so far from her own. Glassworks. Mansions beside a river.

Mike took a sip from his glass of beer. "We're nothing to do with the glass business," he said. "My dad runs a dry goods store. We sell clothes, but most other things too. Sewing machines, some kitchen stuff."

She asked him what he had been doing before the war. "I was at college in Indianapolis," he said. "I was studying engineering. They wanted me to finish that first, but two of my friends were enlisting and I thought that if they were going then so should I. You could say that Uncle Sam called." He took another sip of his beer. "But I'll go back after all this is over. It won't be long now."

She seized at this. People clutched at everything – any scrap of comfort they encountered. Rumours abounded: there were new weapons, on our side; the Germans were running out of oil; their own people were rioting because they were even more short of food than we were; somebody was planning to shoot Hitler and the war would come to an end that way. Every fresh story gave a few moments of comfort before being discounted.

"It's not going to be long?" she asked.

He seemed so confident. "No. We're hitting them hard – and your boys are too. That's my job, you see. We fly those planes over and take photographs, so we know what's going on. We're a reconnaissance unit."

She had a slight sense of being made party to information that she should not know, and she changed the subject. "That tune the band's playing – do you know what it is?"

He listened. "'Speaking of Heaven'," he said. "Glenn Miller played it. At least, that's what I think it is."

"I'm bad at songs. I like them, of course, but I get them mixed up."

"I find I remember the words," he said. "It's not much use, of course, because I can't sing. But they stick somewhere up there." He tapped his forehead. *"Speaking of heaven, once I found an angel . . .* and then I forget what comes after that."

She glanced at him. She had been too shy to look at him properly. She lowered her gaze to the glass in her hand. This could not be happening, but it was. And that, they said, was how it always happened: you were not expecting it; and then it happened, and you were in love. Just like that. She thought that was why they used the expression *falling in love*, because it was sudden, and unexpected, as a fall is, and it was very much the same feeling, of sudden powerlessness as gravity took hold of you, as love does; love and gravity were very similar: equally strong, equally irresistible.

Over the two weeks that followed, he saw her eight times: twice when she went to the base to deliver the eggs, and on other occasions when he managed to get a few hours away from the base in the evenings and came to the house in the village. As an officer, he was allowed to be away from the base when not on duty, and his evenings were free as photographic units rarely flew at night. Annie liked him, and would tactfully leave them alone in the small sitting room, on the pretext that she had to go out and Willy would have to accompany her. Willy was bemused, but was won over by a book that Mike gave him on the identification of American planes.

"He's nice, that American pilot," he said. And then, with un-feigned interest, "Do you really like him, Val? Are you sweet on him?"

"I really like him, Willy. He's kind, isn't he?"

"Is he from Texas?"

She smiled. "No, he's from a place called Muncie, Indiana. It sounds like a really nice place. He's shown me some photographs."

He had a camera and what seemed to her to be an unlimited supply of film. He developed this in the same darkroom they used for their reconnaissance shots, and he said there was no cost involved. "I get the film cheap and the chemicals are there anyway, so I slip mine through when the guys finish with the spools from the planes. Nobody minds."

He was generous with his time. He took a portrait photograph of Annie, who dressed especially carefully for the sitting, wearing her best dress, a dress she had not worn for fifteen years: a silk shift in the flapper style. "It makes me look ridiculous," she said. "Mutton dressed up as lamb."

"You could never look ridiculous," he said.

Val liked that. Mike knew what to say, she thought. They said the Americans had good manners, and they were right. Those things they said about Americans boasting and smoking cigars was all invention, she thought. People were jealous because they had tinned peaches and lots of fuel and because they did not look hungry, the way so many English people did.

He took a photograph of Willy in his suit, which was too small for him and pinched about the chest and shoulders. Willy was pleased with the result and framed it, placing it on the chest of drawers in his room. Val wanted to tell him that people did not put up photographs of themselves – it would be considered odd to do so – but then realised that perhaps it was not so odd if you had nobody else to display. And Willy had nobody, unless you counted her and Annie: there were no girlfriends – he was too shy for that – and she knew that the other young men from the village, although kind enough, laughed at him behind his back.

Mike did not. He said, "It's a shame that Willy can't get to the States. He's a hard worker and he could get somewhere in Indianapolis. We have a big plant there that makes medicines. You ever heard of Colonel Eli Lilly?"

"Is he at the base?" Val asked.

Mike laughed. "No, he was a colonel in the Civil War. He came back from the South and started making medicines back home. They built it up and now there's a big place that has hundreds of people working for it. Chemists, doctors even. But there are jobs for all sorts of people. Drivers. Guys who work on the machinery – the tubes and vats and things like that."

"I'm not sure if Willy . . ."

"Maybe not. But if he met a nice girl who could take care of him, he could get by just fine."

She looked at him and knew, at that moment, that if he asked her to marry him, she would accept without hesitation. Muncie, Indiana was a long way away, and there would be things about it that would be strange to her, but that would not matter if Mike was with her. And that was all she wanted: to be with him.

On one occasion, when he was unable to get away from the base, he sent a card to her, delivered by an airman. She opened it in her bedroom, her hands shaking. It was in his handwriting: *To my sweetheart*, it said. *The sweetest girl in England. From Mike, the guy who thinks of her every minute of those longs hours of flying. Every minute.*

She slipped it under her pillow and that night, waking up in the small hours, she took it out, switched on her light, and read it again and again before she tucked it back under the pillow and dropped off to sleep smiling.

It was on a Saturday evening that Willy brought the dog back to the house. Willy worked all day on Saturday – Sunday was his only day off – but he came back on this occasion slightly earlier than usual. Annie was listening to the wireless and Val was cooking when he came into the kitchen and announced that there was something outside he wanted them to see. Annie asked if it could wait – her programme had twenty minutes to run – but Willy said that it would be best if they came right away.

The dog was in the small garden behind the post office, tied to a leg of the wooden bench on which Annie sat in fine weather.

Annie exchanged glances with Val, who rolled her eyes. "Whose dog is this, Willy?" she asked. She thought that she already knew the answer, but asked the question anyway.

"It's one of the dogs from the farm. He's the young one. His mother is the one he uses for the sheep."

Annie nodded. "I thought as much. And why is he here, Willy?"

Willy said nothing for a while, but then he burst out with his explanation. It was a torrent of words, a rambling imprecation.

"He beat him this morning. I saw him. He told me to mind my own business, but he hit him with a stick because he'd been barking. So I've brought him here. I knew you wouldn't mind – and please say it'll be all right. Butters went off somewhere with one of his pals and I was there by myself, so I untied him and brought him here. I left a note for him on the kitchen table. I said, *Your dog's run away and I don't know where he is.* I said that

I'd look for him and bring him back if I saw him, but I won't. So can he stay here, Auntie? Please. He wants to stay – I can tell he does. I'll feed him and he'll be no trouble."

He drew breath once he had finished and looked at her imploringly. Annie bent down to pat the dog's head. He whimpered, and tried to lick her hand.

"You see," said Willy. "He likes you already."

She straightened up. "We can't have a dog, Willy. You're out all day long and I'm busy in the post office. I can't take him in there. You know that."

"He'd be no trouble. He's not a noisy dog. He's very quiet."

Val moved forward. "He could come to Archie's farm. He used to have a dog. He said something the other day about missing him."

Annie frowned. "You'd have to ask him first."

"I'll take him with me on Monday and see what he says. Will he run alongside a bike?"

Willy told them that this was how he had brought him home. "He's got strong legs. You tie a bit of string to his collar and he'll run beside the bike for miles. Give him a rest now and then, but otherwise he's fine." He looked at Annie. "So, can he stay until then – just two nights?"

Annie sighed. "One more mouth to feed, I suppose. But we can't turn him out." She bent down to pat the dog once more. "Has he got a name?"

"Peter Woodhouse," said Willy.

Val laughed. "Peter Woodhouse? That's a grand name for a dog."

Willy looked defensive. "That's what's written on the side of his kennel. It's on one of the boards. It says Peter Woodhouse."

Annie burst out laughing. "Woodhouses were a firm of removers. They used to pack people's furniture in crates. Peter Woodhouse. That's where it comes from – it's an old Woodhouse crate. That's what his kennel is made of."

"Well, that's what I call him anyway," said Willy. "And he answers to it. You try."

"Dogs answer to anything," said Val. "If you called out Winston Churchill, I bet he'd answer."

"It's a good name for him," said Annie. "Let him be Peter Woodhouse."

Permission was given, and the dog spent the night on an old rug under the kitchen table. In the morning, he awoke the household by scratching at the door, and it was Annie who took him out into the garden. Then she fed him with a bowl of porridge mixed with a small amount of chicken's liver that a friend had given her.

"It's going to be a new life for you, Peter Woodhouse," she said. "Your war's over now."

Archie took it in his stride. He was standing in the doorway of one of the barns when he saw her ride down the track with the dog trotting beside her.

"So, you got yourself a dog," he said as she drew up and dismounted in front of him.

She leaned her bike against the wall of the barn. "My cousin rescued him," she said. "He was being mistreated."

"Nice-looking animal," said Archie. "Reminds me a bit of my last dog."

Val took advantage of this. "Then you wouldn't mind if he stayed here?" she said. "He's had a miserable time."

"Hold on," said Archie. "I didn't say I wanted a dog."

"No, but he wants you. Look at the way he's gazing up at you. Look at that. He thinks the world of you already, I'm sure he does."

She could see that it was working. Archie was ruffling the fur around the dog's neck.

"You're a good fellow, are you?" he said. "A good watchdog? Bark at any ne'er-do-wells who come around the place, will you?"

This was her chance. She knew that farmers were worried by theft. For people in towns, worn down by queues for rations that seemed to get smaller and smaller, the temptation to help themselves to a chicken or a duck was sometimes just too great. "He's good at that," said Val. "You know how Mrs Carter lost ten of her chickens the other night? They traced them from the feathers. They were on the ground, all the way down to that army camp. Right into the barrack room where the lads who stole them were living. They would have caught them red-handed, if they hadn't already sold the chickens."

"Heard about it," said Archie. "A bad business."

"Well, Peter Woodhouse wouldn't let that happen."

Archie looked puzzled. "Peter Woodhouse?"

"That's his name," said Val. "It's a pretty unusual name for a dog, but it suits him somehow."

Archie sucked in his cheeks. "He'd need to be fed."

"Rabbits," said Val quickly. "Teach me how to shoot and I'll get them myself."

"I'll do it," said Archie. "I can fix him up with a rabbit. Last him a week, a rabbit will."

She realised now that she had won.

"I'll find something for his kennel," she said. "A box, perhaps . . ."

Archie had already thought of that. "There's an old wooden crate in the barn. It's got something in it, but I'll clear it out. That'll do fine."

On impulse, she turned round and kissed the farmer on the cheek. He looked flustered.

"Sorry," she said. "It's just that you're so kind and I thought I might give you a kiss. It's really from Peter Woodhouse, not from me."

"Nothing wrong with a dog's kiss," said Archie gruffly. "My old dog used to kiss me when I let him loose each morning. He jumped up and was all over me. Great wet kisses all over my face. Never did me any harm."

They looked for the wooden crate together, and Val watched as Archie cut a door in the front and nailed planks together to make a roof, over which he pinned sacking to provide protection against rain. Then they moved the crate into position near the kitchen door – the best place for a dog to be, Archie said, "so that he doesn't feel left out".

She had been putting off the moment when she would tell him where the dog came from. But now, with Peter Woodhouse introduced to his kennel and already lying down on the sacking bedding inside – the long run from the village had caught up with him – she broached the subject.

"My cousin Willy gave him to me," said Val. "He took him from his last owner. He beat him."

Archie was not paying much attention. "Oh yes?" he said vaguely.

"He was one of Ted Butters' dogs."

This brought a reaction. "He belonged to Ted Butters? Over at Craig Hill?"

Val nodded. "Willy works over there. He says he treats his dogs terribly. Beats them. That's why he took this one away from him."

For a while, Archie was silent. Then he asked, "Does Butters know?"

"No, he doesn't."

Archie stroked his jaw. "There's no need for him to know," he muttered. "Can't stand people who treat dogs badly. Never could."

Val felt relieved. "He'll assume he strayed. Dogs do that."

Archie agreed. "Keep it to yourself," he said. "If nobody knows, Butters won't ever find out. That man! Disgrace to farming, he is."

Val knew then that she had an ally, and Peter Woodhouse, who had been at the mercy of a bully and a tyrant, now had two allies too. It was like the war, she thought: small countries who had been bullied had discovered there were big friends willing to fight for them. It was enough to make anybody believe that there was such a thing as justice – somewhere in the inner workings of the world, in the mechanisms of human affairs, there was justice.

The dog settled in quickly. At lunchtime on that first day, Val left her work cleaning out the hen houses to check up on him in the yard. He greeted her effusively, and she untied him to let him explore his new surroundings. Archie called her in for lunch – he had heated a pot of leek soup – and from the kitchen window they both watched Peter Woodhouse running around the farmyard, sniffing at everything and getting to know his new home.

"I've got some stew for him," said Archie. "I'll call him in."

He went to the door and shouted the dog's name. Peter Woodhouse hesitated, uncertain what to do – a call in the past might have been the prelude to a beating, but he sensed now that things were different, and he came trotting over to the kitchen door. Rewarded with a large bowl of stew, which he wolfed down with all the urgency with which dogs attack their meals, he was allowed to join them in the kitchen. There he wasted no time in finding a spot near the wood-fired cooking range, stretched himself out, and was soon half asleep. One eye remained fractionally open, though, in the way that dogs will have it when they are keen to keep at least some sort of watch on what is happening around them.

"The thing to remember," reflected Archie, "is that these creatures are pack animals. Understand that, and you understand a dog."

"They need a leader," said Val.

"Yes, they need a leader. And that's why they put up with people who are unworthy of them – like that Ted Butters. He's the man in charge, you see, and they just accept it. You never get dogs arguing about that sort of thing. Even dogs over in them communist countries. They don't go around having revolutions and what-not."

Val laughed. She had begun to see a dimension to Archie that she had been unaware of at the beginning, when she had first started working on his farm. He was just a farmer then – a taciturn middle-aged man who liked things done in a particular way and seemed to be content enough with his own company; but slowly he had revealed his sense of humour and his kindness, and she was heartened by both.

6

Mike said, "I guess you're my girl now." He blushed. "I find it kind of hard to say these things, but you know what I mean."

They were sitting in the pub in the village. There were few people there: a couple of the girls from the land girl house, waiting for some young men from the RAF base; two farm hands, still in working clothes, their trousers tied with binding twine just above the ankles; a lonely-looking man in a sports jacket and tie, reading the racing page of the paper. Val and Mike were far enough away from anybody to be able to talk without lowering their voices, and to hold hands without attracting attention.

She looked down at the floor, and then up again, to meet his gaze. She liked to see him blushing; it was a curious, boyish thing – almost a matter of manners.

"I'm happy with that," she said. "I like being your girl."

He squeezed her hand. "When all this is over . . ."

She sighed. "We say that all the time, don't we? *When this is over* . . . But somehow I wonder whether it ever will be, or whether it will just go on and on and we'll . . ."

He interrupted her. "It'll be over, and then I'll take you back to the States with me. Would you like that?"

She felt her heart beating. Willy had asked her that morning whether Mike had proposed to her yet. He had said, "He'll want you to marry him, I bet. Any time now, he'll ask you."

She had told him not to be ridiculous, but his words had thrilled her. Of course she had thought about it – any girl going out with a man at least thought about the possibility, unless, of course, she was purely out for a good time; for tinned peaches, as her aunt would say. And there were girls like that; girls who were out to get what they could without any thought as to the man's feelings.

Now he was talking about her going to America, and how could that be seen as anything but a proposal?

"What would I do in America?" she asked. She knew that she sounded teasing; she did not intend it, but she did.

He hesitated for a few moments before answering. "I'd look after you."

"We'd go to Muncie, Indiana?"

He squeezed her hand again. "Anywhere you want. We could go out west if you liked. Los Angeles, maybe. I could get a job there, now that I have this experience of aerial photography."

She wished that he would ask her directly. Why could he not just say, *Will you marry me?* She would say yes to that question. It was what she wanted.

"I wouldn't mind going to America," she said.

He leaned over towards her and planted a gentle kiss on her cheek. One of the land girls, still waiting for their RAF boyfriends, noticed, and flashed a smile of encouragement.

"Then we're engaged," he said. It was not a question; it was a statement of fact, and she nodded her assent. She did not say anything, although she tried. It was too difficult for her because she found herself not thinking of him, or even of herself, but of her mother and of how she would have approved of him; she had approved of everything her daughter did, right from the beginning. She had never thought her daughter anything less than wonderful.

She realised that he had said something about a ring. "I'm sorry, I was thinking."

It seemed as if he understood. "Of course. It's a big thing, isn't it – getting engaged and then getting married."

Getting married . . . She closed her eyes.

He said, "There's a guy at the base can get hold of rings from the States. He knows somebody in the business. He can order them."

"That would be lovely." It was all she could think of to say.

"I need to know the size of your finger. He has a card, this guy, and you put your finger into the hole that fits. Then you know the right size."

She laughed at the thought. "You Americans think of everything, don't you?"

But now a shadow passed over her face, and he saw it. He asked gently if something was wrong. "You don't have to say yes, you know. The last thing I'd want to do is to make you say yes. You know that, don't you?"

She reassured him that she had said yes freely, and that she meant it. She did not reveal to him, though, what her thoughts had been, because they had been of the path of danger into which he flew every day, or almost every day. She had seen a plane limping home, a trail of smoke – not wide, but visible – issuing from an engine. Even if they were just taking photographs, they were flying over the heads of people who would be trying to bring them down, and who from time to time – probably rather often – succeeded in doing so. There were legions of young women who had become engaged to men who were risking their lives in this way and had learned that the game of dice their menfolk played had gone against them. One of the land girls on another farm was in this position; Val had seen her, and she had been tearful. One of the other girls had whispered the explanation: her fiancé of two weeks had been shot down somewhere and now she had been notified officially that he was dead.

"I don't want to lose you," she said.

He laughed. "Nobody's going to take me away from you. Nobody." And then, with an expression of mock bravado, "Let them try!"

It suddenly occurred to her that there were young women on the other side thinking the same thing about their men, and their men would be saying the same words back to them. It was the men who started it, she thought. Left to women, it would not work out this way; they would ground the planes that took their lovers from them; they, and the mothers, would put a stop to war.

That was a thought that Annie had often expressed, but no sooner had she done so than she had admitted that men were needed to fight evil. "Hitler wouldn't listen to us women," she said. "There's only one thing that Hitler understands."

Mike was looking at his watch. She did not dare ask him whether there was a mission that day; she assumed there was.

"I have to get back to the base," he said. He looked at her. "I'll be thinking of you tonight. I have to go out with a bomber tonight. They're short of men."

Her heart gave a leap. Not all bombers came back; everyone knew that. They were lumbering and defenceless, people said, and the men who flew them simply had to grit their teeth, do their job, and hope that they dodged the flak thrown up at them.

"You must be really careful."

"Yes. Of course I will. In and out. Back to base."

"And I'll be thinking of you too. Always. All the time."

He put his fingers to her lips. "Promise?"

She moved his fingers gently, and placed them where she imagined her heart was. "Promise."

7

"I ain't going back," said Willy. "I don't care if they shoot me – I ain't going back there."

Annie attempted to calm him. She had seen how he could get worked up, and she knew it could end with him in tears, sobbing his heart out over something that any normal young man would treat as minor.

"Hush, Willy. Hush. Nobody's going to shoot you." She glanced at Val, who rolled her eyes.

"They don't shoot people who leave their jobs," said Val.

Willy stared at her, his bottom lip quivering. "This is wartime. It's different in wartime. They can shoot you if you disobey."

"That's in the army," said Val. "And only if you run away from the enemy."

"And not any longer," added Annie. "That was in the first war – at the Somme and places like that. The army's more civilised now. They don't shoot their own men." She was not sure about that; she thought they probably did, but she was not going to give Willy yet another thing to worry about.

Willy looked unconvinced. "Anyway, I don't care. They can't make me go back to Ted Butters' place."

They were standing in the kitchen. Willy had just returned from work early – usually he arrived half an hour or so after Val, but he had come in before that, his hair dishevelled and his expression agitated. Now, Annie suggested they all sit down at the kitchen table and Willy could tell them exactly what had happened.

"So just calm down," said Annie. "Calm down and tell us what went wrong. From the beginning."

"I went to work on his farm," said Willy. "I started four months ago. He told me —"

Annie reached out to put her hand on his arm. "No, Willy, not that beginning. From today, this morning. What happened today that made you come back early?"

"It was the rats," said Willy. "Them rats in his haystack. They made a big nest like they always do. Pa rat, Ma rat and all their nippers."

"Kittens," supplied Val. "They call the little rats kittens. They have litters, same as cats do."

"I knew they were there," Willy continued. "They weren't doing any harm. He didn't have to kill them."

Annie sighed. "Farmers do, Willy. They kill rats because they eat food that's meant for livestock. And if the farmer grows grain too – oats and barley and so on – rats love that for their tea."

"Auntie's right," said Val. "Archie lays poison for rats. He says they steal his eggs. And they do – I've seen eggs broken by rats. You can see the tooth marks."

"These rats were doing none of that," persisted Willy. "They were minding their own business. They weren't in the barn." He paused. "And I wanted to take one of them. A rat can be a friendly creature – same as a small dog, they say."

This brought a response from Annie. "I'm not having rats around here," she warned. "Not for anything. Nasty creatures, with those long tails of theirs, and their teeth."

Willy ignored this. "He hit them with a shovel," he said. "All of them – the whole family."

Annie exchanged a concerned glance with Val. "You didn't . . ."

He cut her short. "I didn't hit him, if that's what you're

worried about. But I told him what I thought of him."

Annie breathed a sigh of relief. "Well, he probably knew that already."

Willy smiled. There was a sly satisfaction in his look. "He didn't like it, he didn't. I told him that he didn't deserve to have any animals. I told him that his dog hadn't run away: I'd taken him. He didn't like that neither."

Val frowned. "You told him you'd taken Peter Woodhouse? Did you tell him where he is, Willy?"

Willy did not seem to appreciate the gravity of the situation. "I told him he had a much better home over at Archie Wilkinson's place."

Val suppressed a cry of dismay. "Oh, Willy . . ."

"He didn't like that," crowed Willy. "You should have seen his face. He went all purple. Ted Butters gets purple when he gets cross." He sniffed. "He said I should go and not bother to come back. I told him I didn't want to come back, but what about the money he owed me? A full week's wages. He said I could do what I like but he'd never pay me. He said if I didn't clear off he'd fetch his shotgun."

Annie glanced again at Val, and shook her head slightly. "You can't be blamed, Willy. You should never have been sent to that man in the first place. You're well away from him."

He seemed reassured. "They'll find me some other place?"

"Of course they will," said Annie. "There are plenty of farms needing somebody."

"And the army won't take me?"

"No, the army won't take you. They told you that, remember? They said that you were better working on a farm." She paused, once more glancing conspiratorially at Val. "You know what I reckon, Willy? I think that if they told Mr Churchill himself about the work you do on the land, he'd say *Well done, William Birks*. That's what he'd say, Willy. Mr Churchill himself."

He rubbed his hands together with pleasure. "It's what I do best. It's what I do best to help win the war."

Annie was soothing. "Of course it is, Willy. And now, why don't you go and have a bath before I serve your tea. There's a clean shirt in your cupboard – I ironed it this morning. You put that on."

Once Willy had left the kitchen, Val shook her head in disbelief. "I can't believe he doesn't understand. It's so basic. He told that Ted Butters to his face where Peter Woodhouse is. Now what?"

Annie sighed. "You tell Archie tomorrow that he has to find somewhere safe for the dog. There'll be plenty of time. Ted Butters won't do anything this evening. So put the dog some place where he'll not be found. Let the whole thing blow over."

"But what if it doesn't?"

"It will – it'll blow over. Ted Butters is too busy with his black market activities to spend time making a fuss over a dog."

"Black market?"

"He sells chickens. Sometimes a pig. He sells to that Martin Crowhurst and his friends. They'll be caught one day."

Val told her aunt that one of the men at the base had been caught stealing the Americans' supplies and selling them on the black market. He was going to prison.

"Best place for Ted Butters," said Annie.

The following morning Val arrived at the farm half an hour earlier than usual. Archie was still at the kitchen table, nursing a large mug of tea and reading a farming leaflet. She knocked at the kitchen window and was invited in.

"Has something happened?" he asked.

"Nothing. Well, something has, I suppose. Ted Butters knows that Peter Woodhouse is here."

Archie raised an eyebrow. He did not seem overly concerned. "How did he work that out?"

She told him, stressing that Willy was not entirely responsible for his actions. "He understands some things," she said. "But he doesn't always work things out the same as you and I do."

"So I see," said Archie. "But no use crying over spilt milk."

"No." She paused. "What do you think Ted Butters will do?"

Archie shrugged. "He might come round here. If he does, I'll tell him the dog has voted with his feet. I'll tell him there'll be no taking him back."

She was concerned that the other farmer might create trouble. Archie nodded. "Yes, there's always that, I suppose. But I'll deal with any trouble he makes. He has a foul temper on him, that man, but I've dealt with the likes of him before."

She was reassured. "So we do nothing?"

"We carry on," said Archie. "Isn't that what they're always telling us – the government, that is? Carry on, they say. Well, that's what we'll do." He swigged the rest of his tea and then rose from the table. "We've got half a field of cabbages to get in while this weather holds, my girl. Let's not waste any time."

They went to work. At eleven in the morning, they stopped for a short break, and that was when they saw Bill Edwards coming up the farm track on his ancient black bicycle. The policeman waved to them and then parked his bike against a hedge at the bottom of the cabbage field. Picking his way around the side of the field he came to join them.

"Well, Bill?" said Archie. "You looking for a German spy or something? Nobody round here, I'm afraid."

The policeman smiled. "You checked your hayloft recently, Archie? It's a great place for a German spy to hide up.'

"I'll do as you say, Bill," said Archie.

The policeman cleared his throat. He was still sweating from the ride up from the village, and now he wiped his brow with a large red handkerchief. "Actually, Archie," he began, "it's a tricky one. I've had a visit from Ted Butters. You know him?"

"Of course I do," said Archie. "Not that I'd describe him as a friend."

"There's a lot would say that," said the policeman. "I keep out of these scraps, obviously, but I hear what people are saying – and thinking too, sometimes – and I know who's popular and who isn't. Not that I'm saying anything about it, mind."

Archie nodded. "Of course not."

"Anyway," continued the policeman, "Ted Butters comes round to see me first thing this morning and lays a complaint that you've stolen his dog. He says it's worth six pounds, being a highly trained sheepdog."

"A good dog's not cheap," said Archie.

Bill Edwards looked embarrassed. "You can't turn a blind eye to the taking of a dog worth six pounds," he said. "That's the same thing as stealing a horse. Just as valuable."

"I suppose so," said Archie. "But nobody's stolen that Butters' dog. He mistreated it, by the way; he beat it something terrible. A dog won't stand for that, you know; a dog will try to get away."

Bill Edwards pursed his lips. "A dog doesn't run away by itself. Dogs stay. I've had dogs myself."

"Some dogs do," insisted Archie. "It all depends on the dog."

Bill fiddled with the policeman's helmet he was holding. "You wouldn't happen to have this dog on your farm, would you, Archie? I'm asking you directly, see, as a friend, so to speak."

Archie hesitated, but then he gave his response. "It's here, Bill, because the poor creature was being beaten to death up at Butters' place. We couldn't stand by."

The policeman's embarrassment deepened. "A farmer's dog's different, Archie. You know that. It's part of the farm equipment, so to speak. You can't take it off him."

"I'm not disputing that, Bill," said Archie. "But there's the dog to think of here. A dog's not like other . . . bits of property. A dog's different."

The policeman shifted his weight from foot to foot. "I don't want to make a fuss about this, Archie, but if a complaint's been made . . ." He gave the farmer an imploring look. "Of course, if the dog were to go somewhere else for a while, then I could truthfully inform Butters that there's no dog here. I'll come back officially tomorrow – this is an unofficial visit, you'll understand – and there'll be no dog and that'll be the end of it as far as I'm concerned."

Archie smiled. "You're a good man, Bill," he said. "We'll make sure there's no dog for . . . for your official visit."

They watched him ride down the road back towards the village.

"That's the way a policeman should behave," said Archie. "There's always a solution if you're prepared to be flexible."

8

If they could manage it, the time Mike and Val had together, precious hours snatched between the claims of flying and working on the farm, was spent away from others. Wartime was a period of constant sharing with people you did not know – in bomb shelters, in overcrowded public transport, in the endless queueing for almost everything. To be alone with another, to talk without fear of being overheard, seemed at times to be an impossible, only dimly remembered luxury, almost an act of selfishness.

After completing a spell of intensive duties, he was given two days' leave. He wanted to go away – to drive off with her in a car lent by one of the other pilots – but it was a busy time on the farm and she felt unable to ask for two full days off. One day at the most, she said, would be all that she could manage.

He said that in wartime you had to take what you could get. The weather was fine and they could take a picnic; he would still get the use of the car and they could go wherever she suggested.

"I know a place," she said. "There's a river, and a bank that will be ideal for a picnic. Sometimes people swim there, but most of the time there's nobody."

He said, "I have some . . ."

"Tinned peaches?"

He laughed. "Yes."

Tinned peaches had become a private joke, because she had told him about Annie's craving for them and he had already supplied a few tins for her. "What's it with you people and tinned peaches?" he asked. "Tinned peaches are just . . ." He shrugged his shoulders. "Just tinned peaches."

"I know that. But there's something about . . ."

"Something about tinned peaches?"

She smiled. She loved him so much; she was sure of it now. Love came to you on the coat-tails of such small things – conversations about tinned peaches, looks exchanged at odd moments, the way that the other person glanced up at the sky, or scratched his head, or said something about the weather. "Yes," she said. "Maybe it's because we could never get them. You really want the things you can't get, don't you?"

He kissed her. They were standing outside the post office and there were people about, but she did not mind. Some people did not like the way the Americans flirted with the local girls, but most did not feel that way. And if those who did not like it should choose to talk, what difference did it make? People disapproved of the things they had themselves missed; Annie had pointed that out to her once and she realized that it was quite true. "If somebody shakes their head and tut-tuts," she said, "you can be sure it's because they wanted to do whatever they're shaking their head and tut-tutting over."

"So," he said. "Tinned peaches. And what else?"

She thought for a moment. "Sandwiches. A picnic isn't a picnic without sandwiches."

"What sort?"

She answered without hesitation. "Oh, ham, I'd say. And egg. And maybe cucumber." She paused. "Yes, cucumber. That's what Annie gives the vicar when he calls round: cucumber sandwiches. The vicar tucks into a whole plate of them – and eats the lot. Every one of them."

"I suppose it's part of his job," said Mike. "I think that you have to eat things in some jobs. We have a congressman back in Indiana who's really fat. He said something in the newspaper about how it all came from his job – visiting folks' houses and having to eat their cookies and cakes or they won't vote for you. It's tough."

Val smiled vaguely; she was thinking of their picnic. "I don't think we've got any ham . . ."

"Leave it to me," said Mike.

"We've got plenty of eggs," said Val, brightening. "And cress. We grow that."

"Then that's our picnic fixed," said Mike.

He leaned forward and kissed her again. As he did so, she thought: *Don't fly ever again. Stay with me. We'll run away together. Anywhere. Anywhere. The war can get on with itself – it doesn't need us.* But she knew that was wrong, even as the thought came to her. This was their war and they had to see it through. He flew a plane and she dug potatoes and carrots: two different ways of fighting the same war.

They found the place by the river, but only after taking a few wrong turnings and having to reverse down impossibly narrow lanes, bounded by out-of-control hedgerows. With people being too busy growing food, there was little time for the luxury of hedge-trimming, and here and there unbridled growth from either side met above a road, making a tunnel, a green womb of dappled light and startled birds. At length Val saw a road she recognized and they found the lay-by where the car could be left. From there, a path followed the edge of a field of ripening wheat down towards a copse of willow trees and the river bank.

She remembered the spot from when she had last been there, just after the war had started. She had come with three other young women, cycling over from the village, a journey of almost ten miles. It had been a hot day, and they had swum in the river, just beneath the lip of a weir, allowing the cooling water to cascade over them like a shower. Then they had lain in the sun, waiting for their bedraggled hair to dry, with one of them keeping watch in case any of the boys from the village should arrive. There was a story – and nobody knew if it was true – about how boys would steal the clothes off swimmers and then hide in the bushes to witness the commotion.

She pointed to a spot shaded by one of the willows, and he laid down the rug he had brought from the car. They embraced.

She said, "I don't want you to go."

He touched her forehead lightly. "I don't want to go either. But I can't . . ." He shrugged. What was the word? Desert? There had been a deserter at the base, a young man from Kentucky who had travelled to London and been picked up by the military police in a bar, drunk and in the company of a woman he had met on the streets of Soho. He had been sent back to the States and to prison.

She sighed, and took his hand in hers. "No, I know you have to do what you're doing. And I wouldn't want to marry a coward."

He looked at her, and wondered whether people who did not go up in planes, who did not face enemy fighters and flak, knew what that particular terror was like. Of course, you could not allow yourself to think about it, and certainly not to talk about it. You had to behave as if you felt none of it, as if you didn't care what happened, while all the time it was always there within you – a cold, hard knot of fear that settled in your stomach and could make you want to retch; only retching solved nothing because the fear would soon return.

She sensed his doubt over what she had said. "Of course, I wouldn't call people cowards if they simply couldn't take it. I know how difficult it must be."

He lay back on the rug, looking up at the sky. "I've not met any cowards," he said. "Not one. I've met people who have cried their eyes out because of everything – sitting there crying their eyes out because . . . well, I guess because they don't want to die, or because they're thinking about the guy they shot down, or something like that. I've met them, but I've never met a coward."

"No," she said. "I'm sure you haven't. I shouldn't have said it."

"No, you can say it, because there is such a thing, and because I can think of times when I've been a coward."

She stared at him. She wished she had never mentioned the word.

"Can I tell you about it?" he asked.

She nodded her head.

"Because," he went on, "I've been thinking about this . . . this thing a lot recently. I don't know why." He paused. "Maybe it's just that when you know that at any moment . . ." He stopped himself. You did not discuss that possibility – especially with your girl.

Of course, she knew what the unspoken words would have been. She looked into his eyes. "Yes," she began, and then trailed off.

"Anyway," he continued, "I've been thinking of something I did when I was a boy – something I'm ashamed of."

She tried to make light of it. "Who hasn't done things they're ashamed of – lots and lots of things – when they were young? Who?"

He shrugged. "Maybe no one."

"Well, there you are."

"Except I can't get this out of my mind. I say to myself, you were just a kid, it was a long time ago, and I wait for that to work. But it doesn't."

At first, she said nothing; she was thinking now of how committing to a joint future brought two pasts together. She realised that she had not given much thought to what marriage meant – how could you think about such things when the world was topsy-turvy with conflict? You could not. But now she thought: *I'm taking on another person's memories, another person's family, another person's life.* Love obscured all of that because if it did not, then nobody would marry at all, and there had to be marriage, didn't there, if people wanted to continue, have children, keep everything going . . .

"I shouldn't bother you with all this," he said. "There are other things to talk about."

She reassured him. "No, you should, because I want you to talk to me. We shouldn't have any —"

"Secrets?" he interjected, smiling. "Isn't that what they say? You don't have any secrets from the person you're going to marry?"

She chided him. "I'm being serious."

He thought for a moment. "Okay."

Val waited. Somewhere in the distance there was a shout,

answered by another – boys playing along the river. A cuckoo calling. A breeze in the leaves of the trees. The vague sound that heat made.

"There was a kid at school," Mike said. "He was called Jimmy Clark. We called him Stan – after Stan Laurel, because he looked a bit like him, and walked like him too. We laughed at him – everybody laughed at him. He was, well, sort of uncoordinated. Clumsy. You know that sort of kid?"

Val thought of a girl she had known at school who was always losing things and getting into trouble as a result. She nodded.

"This guy, this Jimmy Clark, didn't have many friends. In fact, he probably had none. He used to ask people if they would be his friend – he asked me once, I remember – and although people didn't exactly say no, they never really hung around with him. People were kind of embarrassed, if you see what I mean."

"Children are like that, aren't they?"

"Yes, but this went on all the way through high school."

She sighed. "I suppose that's the way it goes."

"He admired me," said Mike. "I was in the football team. I guess I found it easy to make friends."

"He looked up to you?"

"Yes, I think so." Mike paused. "He asked me to go to his place and see this model railway set-up his dad had made. His father was one of these railway enthusiasts who collect model trains – engines, track, the lot. They make a big thing of it. And Mr Clark had made this whole system, it seemed – tunnels, the works."

"You saw it?"

Mike shook his head. "No. I said I was too busy, because . . ." He faltered before continuing. "I didn't want people to think that I was friendly with Jimmy Clark, who was a real loser who still played with trains."

She looked at him, and saw pain in his eyes. But it was such a little thing, she thought; such a little thing. And her heart went out to him: that he should fret over a small unkindness of childhood. He should not; no, she was proud that he should care about something that all of us must have done at some time or other because we were young and thoughtless. "You shouldn't blame yourself for that," she said. "It wasn't such a big thing."

"I haven't told you what happened."

She caught her breath.

"I heard that he enlisted. After I joined the air force, I heard that Jimmy Clark enlisted in the army. He was put into the dental corps. He helped the dentist, I suppose. You know, with the instruments and the mouthwash and so on."

Val said that she thought that must have been important. "You always need dentists, even when there's a war going on."

"Of course," agreed Mike. "Of course it was important. Toothache's toothache. We've got a dentist at the base."

"So that's what happened to him?"

Mike looked away. "Until he was killed, yes."

She closed her eyes. It was the way wartime stories ended.

"He was somewhere in the Pacific. I heard from my aunt, who reads everything in the local paper and sends me cuttings. She sent me the report. There was a picture of Jimmy, and the article just said that he'd been killed on active duty. There was a picture of his mom and dad too. The report quoted them.

They said how proud they were of their son. Then the paper said that he would be much missed by his friends."

Val reached out to take his hand. "Oh, Mike," she whispered.

"Missed by his friends . . . me?" He turned back to face her. "You see how I feel?"

"Yes, of course I do. But you shouldn't dwell on this. You didn't know."

"Didn't know that he was going to go off and get himself killed? In the dental corps? No, of course I didn't, but I don't think that made me feel any better. I could have been his friend. I could have gone to his place to see that damn railtrack. I could have done *something*. But I didn't."

"But it's the war that makes everything, well, rather worse. It's not you, Mike. It's the war."

He shook his head. "It makes me think that you should never not say what you need to say."

"No."

"So, I love you, Val. I love you so much."

She made an effort at cheerfulness. "What will our house be like? Our house in Muncie, Indiana?"

He smiled. "Really neat."

"With a garden?"

"Yes. A garden. Trees. Flowers in the summer. Anything you like."

"And a car?"

He laughed. "Of course. I'll teach you how to drive. Our roads are much straighter than yours. Wider, too."

"So I won't hit anything?"

"Not if you drive straight."

They ate their sandwiches. They walked along the river bank

to where the boys they had heard earlier on were swimming. They had a dog in the water with them, and the dog was fetching sticks.

"Could we take a dog with us to America?" she asked.

He looked doubtful. "I don't think so. I don't think you can take a dog." He looked at her fondly. "You shouldn't worry too much about dogs. Dogs have their own lives, you know."

She knew that. "But their lives get all tangled up with ours," she said.

He agreed. "It's what they want, I think."

"Even in our wars?"

He had not thought about that, but she was right, he decided.

They turned back. One of the boys shouted from the water. "Good luck, mister! Kill the Germans, mister!"

"They're just boys," said Val.

9

When Bill Edwards had gone, Archie said to Val, "Can you take that dog back to your aunt's place, just for the time being? A week or two – maybe a bit longer."

Val thought about this. Annie had a kind heart, but her situation was awkward. Everybody went to the post office from time to time – including Ted Butters. Ted's cousin, Alice, lived a couple of houses away. She and Ted were on good terms and she would probably recognise the dog easily enough. They could not risk that now that Bill Edwards was involved.

"It would be better for him to go somewhere else," she said. "You know how it is in the village. People talk – even in wartime, they talk."

Archie understood. "You're right: he must go somewhere else." He looked at her enquiringly. "Any ideas?"

Suddenly it came to her. "Yes," she said. "Mike will take him."

"Your fellow?"

"My fiancé now. Yes. He likes dogs, and he said that somebody at the base had a dog but it ran away."

Archie looked unconvinced. "An air force base is no place for a dog. All that noise. All that coming and going."

"It won't be for long," said Val. "And think of the attention he'll get – and the food."

Archie had to admit the food would be better. "They have steaks down there," he said. "They have steaks the size of which you wouldn't dream of. A dog could get the trimmings and do very well out of them."

Val smiled. "He'd be well fed. The Americans look after their own."

Archie shrugged. "If he'll take him, that's the answer." He paused. "We could drive him there in the van. I've got a drop of petrol."

They went out into the yard. Peter Woodhouse was in his kennel, tied to the wire run that allowed him a certain measure of freedom. He leapt up at Val and licked her hands and arms enthusiastically, reaching her face and covering it with slobbering kisses.

"He knows," she said. "He knows that we're planning something for him."

They drove to the base, taking with them the delivery of eggs that would get them past the guard. Val was known there now, not because of the engagement, which was unofficial, but as a supplier of eggs. Sergeant Lisowski had told the guardroom that she could come and go as she pleased, and she had never encountered any difficulty in getting past the front gate. Now, on this visit, there were a few more questions as Archie was asked who he was, but they were soon waved through.

Because Val did not know whether Mike would be there, she spoke to Sergeant Lisowski.

"The lieutenant's on a mission," he said. "Just left."

She explained about Peter Woodhouse, without mentioning the real reason why refuge was needed. "We can't look after him right now," she said. "I wondered if Mike could take him."

Sergeant Lisowski looked down at the dog. "I love dogs," he said. "We had wiener dogs back in Pittsburg. Three of them. They're great dogs. Small bodies, big hearts."

"This is a sheepdog," said Val. "They're not like . . . what did you call them?"

"Wiener dogs. You call them sausage dogs over here," said Sergeant Lisowski. "They're German, but they're not Nazis."

Archie laughed. "Dogs don't know about these things," he said.

Sergeant Lisowski looked momentarily surprised. "I guess they don't." He bent down to pat Peter Woodhouse. "I can take care of this dog, even if the lieutenant doesn't want him. Maybe we can look after him together."

"I'd like that," said Val.

Sergeant Lisowski took the lead they had attached to Peter Woodhouse's collar. The dog looked up at him, and then at Val and Archie; he was clearly confused. Val saw that, and her face fell.

"They know when we're abandoning them," she said. "They can tell."

"He's not being abandoned," said Archie. "I would never abandon a dog."

"No," said Val. 'I'm sorry. We're handing him over temporarily."

"Temporarily," agreed Sergeant Lisowski. "Everything's temporary these days, isn't it? Life itself. Temporary."

It was ten days before she saw Mike again. She had a message, though, left with her aunt at the post office, delivered from the base. It was a short note to tell her that Peter Woodhouse was doing fine. *They call him Woody here,* he wrote. *The base commander has taken a shine to him and says he can be on pay and rations as a mascot. So Uncle Sam is paying for him now! One of the*

*men has gotten hold of a collar from somewhere – a swell new collar
with his name burned into the leather. It suits him just fine.* And
then he ended with the private fondness that made her heart
skip. She loved this man; it was as simple as that. This was a
good, kind man who would take on somebody else's dog, and
was so gentle in everything he did; a gentle boy in the middle
of the great machinery of war.

She told Archie about the note, and he seemed pleased. Bill
Edwards had called round at the farmhouse on his official visit
while Val had been in one of the fields. She had not seen him,
but Archie told her how Bill had made much of looking around
the barn and noting things down in that notebook of his. "He
showed me what he had written," he said. "He wrote: *Inspected
barn: no dog of the description. Inspected farmyard: no dog of the
description.*"

Archie laughed. "I said to him: 'Bill this is a bit of play-acting,
ain't it?' and he shook his head and said, 'Archie, I never told
any lies in my whole police career and I'm not going to start
now. I can show that Ted Butters my notebook and tell him,
face to face, that his dog was not at your farm. I can tell him I
looked. And all of that will be God's truth – every word of it.'"

Val smiled. "It's better not to lie. And you don't want
policemen who lie, do you?"

"If we have that," said Archie, "if we have lying policemen
and all that, then what's the point of this war, I ask you?"

She looked at him. She was thinking of Mike, and of what
he was doing. Why was he here? He was risking his life every
day – or however often it was that he went on those missions
– because he had been told to do it. It was a long way from
Muncie, Indiana, but he had come because it was his duty.

Archie had more to say. "I wonder if they'll take Peter Woodhouse up in their planes. He said he was going to be a mascot. They won't take him with them, will they? For good luck?"

Val said she thought this unlikely. "A plane is no place for a dog. Dogs don't like planes."

This tickled Archie. "Dogs don't like planes? Who told you that, young Val? You ever put a dog in a plane?"

She blushed. "Stands to reason, doesn't it? Dogs don't like loud noises."

Archie disagreed. "Peter Woodhouse hopped up smartly enough on Henry Field's tractor. Remember? When he brought it round, Peter was up there like a rat up a drainpipe. He didn't mind the noise. Wanted to be part of what was going on."

"Tractors and planes are different," said Val. "I don't think dogs like planes. I just think that – I've got no proof."

Mike took her to the local pub when he had his next pass.

"We've been busy," he said. "Your boys have been pounding the Germans and we've been taking pictures of it all." He shook his head. "They won't be able to take much more of this now that we've landed in France. We'll just push on and on until we get to Berlin."

"I want it to end," she said.

"So does everybody. Germans too, I imagine. They're people, after all."

"But Hitler's their fault."

"Sure, he's their fault." He was silent for a few moments. Then he said, "Woody is doing just fine. When do you want him back?"

She had not thought about this, but she explained their concern about Ted Butters. "Someone might tell him again," she said. "We probably need to leave it a little while yet."

Mike seemed pleased. "He fits in well. He obeys orders, you see. Some dogs wouldn't. Sergeant Lisowski had those little dachshunds back in Pittsburg."

"He told us."

"Yes, well, he says that his dogs would never obey orders. He said they'd be court-martialled pretty quickly."

She moved her knee, so that it was touching his under the table. There were fewer opportunities for physical closeness than they would have liked. A war was a public time; private moments were difficult, although people took what chances they could.

Mike took a sip from his glass. He had forced himself to drink the warm beer that had so surprised him at the beginning; now he liked it. "He came with us last time," he said. "You know that? He came in the plane."

She was wide-eyed. "Over there? Over . . . wherever it is you go?"

He nodded. "He whined and whined and the major eventually said *okay, you guys can take him with you.* That was all, and he was great in the plane. We took an old flying jacket for him to lie on and he lay there all through the mission. I held him when we made it back to the base so that he wouldn't get thrown around if it was a rough landing."

"As your mascot?"

"Yeah. A mascot. For good luck."

She asked him whether they would take him again. He replied that they would. "Once you start doing something for good luck, you can't stop it just like that. That's bad luck. So you keep on doing it."

She told Archie the next day. "They're taking Peter Woodhouse up in their planes. He's flying with them."

Archie did not express surprise. "They're quite the boys," he said. "All those air force people are – ours, theirs – they're all the same."

❖ 10 ❖

The colonel sent his clerk to fetch Mike from the officers' mess. It was a summons that everybody dreaded: bad news from home was usually delivered by the colonel himself, who did not believe in delegating unpleasant duties to subordinates. And he did it well, because he was sympathetic – some said the most sympathetic colonel in the US Air Force. That was not the same thing as being soft, they said; he could be as tough as a situation demanded, but he felt for his men and he understood how difficult this war was for so many of them: farm boys who should have been driving tractors rather than flying planes and being killed in Europe.

Mike saluted, and waited for the worst.

"I haven't called you in for bad news," the colonel said quickly. "Nothing like that."

Mike relaxed. He grinned. "That's a relief, sir."

The colonel indicated for him to sit down. "Nor is there any problem with your flying. Nothing but good reports."

"I do my best, sir."

The colonel looked past him, over his shoulder, to where the flag fluttered in the afternoon breeze. A wireless was playing somewhere, and then it was switched off.

"This mascot you guys have taken on – what's his name again?"

Mike smiled. "Peter Woodhouse, sir. He had that name when we took him. We're looking after him for my girl, but he's somehow stayed on."

"No objection to that," said the colonel. "Nice dog. I had setters back in Maine. Irish setters. You know those dogs?"

"I've seen them, sir."

The colonel looked back into the room. "My daddy swore by them. He said you couldn't get a smarter dog in this world than an Irish setter. He bred them, you know, and won all the prizes at the dog shows. When he died I took over his dogs. Four of them. One very old one who never got over his death – pined, you see, pined away to nothing. Had to shoot him eventually because he was just skin and bone and it hurt him too much to walk. A great dog, though."

Mike nodded. "My grandfather had a coon dog on his farm. Nothing special. He was the greediest dog you ever met."

The colonel laughed. "Dogs are always hungry. You show me a dog that's not hungry and I'll tell you you've got yourself a cat by mistake."

Mike looked at his hands: the colonel had not invited him into his office to talk about the merits of different breeds of dogs.

"This dog of yours – I know he's been up in the planes." He looked at Mike over the top of his rimless spectacles, but he was smiling as he spoke. "Don't ever think I don't know what's going on."

Mike nodded. "I'd never say that, sir."

The colonel sat back in his chair. "He likes it?"

"He seems to, sir. He likes being with us. You know how dogs like going in cars and trucks? It's like that. He thinks it's a truck, I guess."

The colonel laughed. "Well, I suppose it feels the same." He paused. "And he doesn't get in the way?"

"Never, sir. Just lies there. Tries to stand up when we land but soon lies down again."

The colonel laughed again. "All right. It's going to have to stop, though. You won't have heard, but I'm being sent down to London for two months. My job here is going to be done by Colonel Harold Mortensen. He's not the easiest man in the air force and . . . well, I'm just making sure that everything is regular before I leave. I don't want him telling anybody that I let people get away with things."

Mike said that he understood.

"So, after next Monday, this . . . what's his name again?"

"Peter Woodhouse."

"This Peter Woodhouse is grounded."

Mike inclined his head in acceptance. "But we can keep him here on the base?"

The colonel made an expansive gesture. "Sure, you can do that. And he can carry on flying until Monday – if he wants."

Mike grinned. "I think he probably will want to," he said.

The colonel looked at his watch. "That's it, Rogers. Leave the door open on your way out. This heat – we're not used to it over here."

Mike passed on the news to his crew and to Sergeant Lisowski, who had taken on responsibility for feeding Peter Woodhouse. They were to fly a mission the next morning, leaving shortly after five, and Mike had the dog's rug brought over to his room so that he could sleep there that night rather than in his kennel behind the cookhouse. It was raining in the morning, but the cloud had lifted by the time they took off, and the sun was already bright on the rooftops of the village when Mike looked down on it. He saw the post office and he thought of Val, wondering whether he should have asked her to be outside, looking up as he flew over her. He had never done that before, and thought that he probably never would. It would be bad luck to do that; doing anything out of the ordinary could tempt providence when the odds were stacked so dangerously against you.

England was a carpet of green beneath them. He saw Cambridge, a smudge of grey lanced by a silver strip: the morning sun was on the river, sending up a shard of light. Then came the blue expanse of the North Sea and, beyond that, the coast of the Netherlands, with its covering of thin mist. Once they were above that, it was mostly water down below, dykes and polders confusing the transition between the sea and the land behind the sea.

His navigator was usually accurate. He knew by dead reckoning where they were and how long it would take them to get to where they wanted to be. But he could also find railway lines and church spires and roads just by looking, reading the landscape below as easily as if it were a map. He now said, "Half an hour, and we'll be there."

They were to photograph Arnhem, which was heavily defended by the occupying Germans. Their pictures would show the position of fortifications and their strength. They had to go over their target quickly, hoping that the anti-aircraft guns would not spot a single plane coming from an unexpected quarter. Conditions were right: a cloudless sky stretched off to the east while the land below was bathed in light. Mike looked up, as he often did before the final approach. He said a prayer, the words a vague jumble of propitiation. There was God and sorry and return; there was Val and mother and home.

On the deck, Peter Woodhouse was half asleep, half awake.

The navigator leaned down and stroked his head, and Peter Woodhouse looked up, licked his hand. Mike half-turned to see this, and smiled.

The navigator slipped his fingers under the collar that they had put on the dog, to check that it was not too tight. He believed that dogs swelled up at altitude and that could make the collar uncomfortable. It needed no adjustment. He looked at the inscription that he had painstakingly burned into the leather with a heated nail, the dots making up the words *Peter Woodhouse, US Air Force, Dog First Class* and giving the name of their base. He was proud of that; it was Peter's identity disc, the token of his membership and service.

Mike pointed to something off their wing: small puffs of smoke appearing in the sky before dissipating quickly, like the birth and rapid death of tiny clouds.

11

Archie explained to Val that there were always more potatoes than one imagined, and that you had to dig deep enough to find them. "You probably know that," he said. "Everyone knows about potatoes."

She did. Annie grew potatoes in the post office garden at the back of the house; where once there had been flowers, vegetables now grew. She had taken out the roses she loved so much and turned some of the ground over to leeks and potatoes, and the Jerusalem artichokes that were now colonising most of the rest. The grocer bought the surplus of those, or exchanged them for beans, of which there sometimes seemed to be too many.

It was hot work. Val had found a hat – a battered straw hat that belonged to Annie but had not been worn for years. It provided some protection, but she felt the rays of the August sun beating down on her back and shoulders. Mike liked her complexion; he said it was paler and softer than that of most girls back home, and he would not want her to burn. She looked about her: a small clump of alders along the edge of the field would give some shade, and she could take her break there.

She was thinking of him. It was only ten days ago that they had become physically intimate. She had thought of that moment again and again and was in awe of its significance. It had changed everything for her. She had given herself to him; she was his. Nothing would ever be the same again; nothing. Annie had sensed it. She had said, "Be careful – that's all I'm going to say to you: be careful." Val had looked away, avoiding her aunt's gaze, but then had turned to her and Annie had put her arms around her and said, "He's made his promise to you – it's all right. It's different for engaged couples, which is what you are. It's allowed, especially in wartime."

Especially in wartime: she knew what that meant, and it made her heart a cold stone within her. The rules were different in wartime because people knew that they could lose each other so easily; everyone was in harm's way, not just those who flew or fought on the ground or at sea. Civilians died in their thousands, bombed in their homes at night, crushed to death by falling masonry, burned in the firestorms of shattered cities.

She tried not to think of that; you couldn't, because if you did you would cry or scream and just make it hard for everybody else. So you worked. You did what you were asked to do, which in her case was to dig potatoes out of the earth and pile them on hessian sacks for Archie to come and collect with a handcart that looked as if it belonged in an agricultural museum.

She took lunch early, when Archie called her into the house. He had made apple juice from his own apples, using his precious sugar to sweeten it, as he knew she had a sweet tooth. Then they listened to the news together: much was said about Montgomery's 21st Army Group. "He won't hang about," said Archie. "He'll tell the men what he wants them to do, and they'll do it. I read that in the papers. They said that Monty always speaks to his men, all the time. That's why they'd do anything for him."

He told her to wait until half past two before going out again. "It won't be so hot then," he said. "And those potatoes are going nowhere." He said she could take some home. "Just one bag, but your aunt will appreciate them, I think, unless she has too many of her own."

"She has some," Val said. "But she won't turn down more. We'll give you some artichokes."

"Blow you up, them artichokes," said Archie, rubbing his stomach.

She worked until half past four, and then took another break, lying on the grass under the alders, looking up at the sky. Mike had told her that they were on a training course for three days, so he would not be up there, up in that dizzy, echoing blue. She blew a kiss up at the sky, that he might collect it when he was next up there; she would tell him it would be waiting for him.

And then she heard Archie calling her. She stood up, dusting her overalls. She looked towards the other side of the field, where the path came up from the farmyard, and she saw Archie, half concealed by the hedge, but now coming into full sight. There was a man with him, a man in uniform, and she thought for a moment that it was Mike. But then, as they approached, she saw that it was Sergeant Lisowski.

She knew immediately from Archie's expression. She closed her eyes. She dug her nails into the palms of her hands. She made herself think of something else; oddly, of her bicycle, that had had a flat tyre on the way home the day before. She saw herself fixing it, dipping the tube into a bowl of water until the tell-tale line of bubbles revealed where the hole was. She asked herself: *Why am I thinking about this when Sergeant Lisowski is coming to speak to me and I know what he's going to say?*

The sergeant supported her on the way back to the farmhouse. Archie walked behind them, awkwardly, unsure what to say. She asked Sergeant Lisowski to repeat what he had said – three times. He told her patiently. He said the plane had not returned. He said that even before it was due to return there had been a message from the RAF. One of their planes had been in the area and had seen a Mosquito go down, an engine on fire. They had not spotted any parachutes and they had seen fire on the ground. They had to assume that the plane had been lost, with both its crew.

She insisted on riding home. They tried to dissuade her, but she brushed them aside and set off, her eyes full of stinging tears. Sergeant Lisowski followed her in his jeep, keeping a discreet distance, but close enough to rescue her when she rode into a ditch and fell off, grazing her right forearm. He loaded the bicycle into the jeep, securing it with a rope. Then he drove her home and delivered her to Annie, who put her hands to her eyes and said, "Oh, my God, I knew it, I knew it."

The colonel came to the post office the next day. His manner was grave, and he spoke to Annie for twenty minutes after he had said what he had to say to Val. He told Annie, "He was a fine young man. He was popular at the base and he was a good flier. It's going to be hard on his family – and on this young lady too, of course."

He then spoke about how wretched war was and how even he had hoped that he would end his air force career without ever seeing the men under his command losing their lives. "But it was not to be. And so I've found out what it is like to send young men off to their deaths. I now know."

Annie said, "We have to do this. We have to see it through, even if we didn't start it."

"You're right," said the colonel. "But does that make it any easier? I'm not sure that it does."

Before he left, the colonel remembered there was something else he had to say. He spoke to Annie about this, because Val had gone to her room, sobbing, and he did not think it would be wise to impart more bad news to her.

"I'm told that the dog we've had as a mascot came from your niece. I'm told it had been her dog."

"Not quite," said Annie. "But we'll find somewhere for him now that Mike . . ."

The colonel interrupted her. "That won't be necessary, m'am. I'm sorry, but the dog was with them on the plane. If you could break that news to your niece, I'd be obliged. I'm very sorry. The men liked that dog."

Willy said to her, "Have you got a photograph of him?"

She stared at him. He had been avoiding her, and at first this had hurt her. But then she came to realise that this was how many people reacted: they did not know what to say and so they kept out of your way. Willy was like that, she thought. Of course he's sorry, of course he knows what I'm feeling, but he has never been in a position like this before and nobody has taught him how to behave. She wanted to say to him, "Willy, all you have to do is show me that you know I'm unhappy, that's all. Hold me when I cry. And cry yourself, if you want to, because you liked him too, and you must feel sad as well."

"Yes, of course I've got a photograph. I took it on his birthday. Remember? He came round here and Auntie made a cake."

He nodded. "I remember that. But I was wondering if you had two photographs. A spare one, see. One you could let me have."

She caught her breath, and nodded. Silently, she fetched

it from the drawer and brought it to him. He examined it, holding it reverentially. "I'll have to cut a bit off – round the edges here." He drew an imaginary line. "So that it'll fit in my frame, you see."

She wanted to kiss him, but he always blushed when Annie tried that, and so she simply reached out and patted his arm. "He liked you a lot, Willy. He said once that it was a pity you couldn't go to Indianapolis. You know that place he talked about? He said you'd do well there."

He was surprised. "Me? Do well?"

"Yes. Of course. He knew you were a hard worker. He said hard workers did well in America."

Willy beamed with pleasure. He looked down at the photograph. "I'll put it in my frame when it's the right size. I'll have his photo in my room. When I wake up in the morning, I'll see that he's all right up there. Like Jesus."

She bit her lip. "That's right, Willy."

Later that day she went to the base to deliver eggs. Archie had said that he would do it, or he could get the neighbour's boy to go, because he was keen to earn a bit of money, but she insisted. "Brave girl," he muttered as he watched her ride down the lane. When she arrived at the base, the young man with angry skin was on sentry duty. He seemed embarrassed and muttered something she did not hear as he let her in. Another man went past on a motorbike, slowed down, and waved to her before moving off again.

Sergeant Lisowski met her at the cookhouse door. He said, "I could come and collect these, you know."

She shook her head. "I want to bring them." She paused. "There's been no news, has there?"

He hesitated. "No, not really. But . . ."

She searched his face for a sign.

He was trying not to give false hope. "When there isn't a definite report, then we assume the worst. But there have been cases – plenty of cases – of people surviving and being taken prisoner. We usually hear one way or another. The Red Cross do their best. We haven't heard on this occasion."

She weighed his words. *Usually . . . this occasion . . . plenty of cases.*

"They could have survived?"

He was being very careful. "It's possible, because . . ."

She waited.

"Because the RAF guys who saw the fire might have been looking at something else. A bonfire, perhaps. There are plenty of reasons for a fire."

There were, she thought. There were plenty of reasons for a fire.

"So I shouldn't give up hope?" Her voice was small.

Again she watched. She would be able to tell if he really meant there was a possibility, or whether he was trying to be kind.

It took him some time to answer. Then he said, "I'd say you could have a tiny bit of hope. A glimmer. But not much more than that."

She mounted her bicycle. She felt that her life was beginning again. She saw a bird, a thrush, watching her from a hedgerow, its tiny head moving jerkily, as birds' heads will do. She shouted at it in sheer exuberant joy.

12

They descended rapidly when the first engine was hit, and the other one quickly overheated. He was surprised at his own calm as he went through all the procedures they had been taught. He did everything in the correct sequence, his only miscalculation being that he might be able to save the plane. By taking it down, he lost the altitude that they needed to bail out, and then it was too late. He still had control of the aircraft, but insufficient power to do anything but attempt a crash landing. He thought, *This is where I'm going to die. Right here, in Holland, and on this day, in five minutes or so. My last five minutes.*

The navigator pointed beyond the starboard wing. It was wooded terrain, but there were some fields, and one had opened up in that direction. He struggled with the controls; the plane was sluggish, but eventually responded to his coaxing and turned in the direction he wanted.

There were saplings, an incipient forest of them, and they hit the plane like tiny whips. Then there was the earth, and the thump and bucking of the undercarriage on rough ground. The plane reared up, shuddered; settled again. Then the wheels hit a ditch traversing the field and they slewed off first to the left and then to the right. Something hit his shoulder a glancing blow, and then, miraculously, they stopped moving. His only thought was that both of them were alive and must leave the plane as soon as they could. He smelled fuel.

There was a whimpering at his knee. They had both forgotten about Peter Woodhouse and he was there, unsteady on his feet, looking up first at Mike and then at the navigator.

They wriggled free of their restraining belts.

"There's blood on your face," said Mike. "All over."

The navigator reached up tentatively. "Something hit my nose," he said. "I think it's broken."

"Get out. We must get out. You first – I'll pass you the dog."

They scrambled out, together with Peter Woodhouse. He tried to lick the blood off the navigator's face, but was pushed roughly away. Now they stood and surveyed the plane from a safe distance. One of the wings had cracked and was at an odd angle to the fuselage. Both propellers were bent, one blade dug into the ground by the engine's dying efforts.

Mike looked at the navigator. He wanted to hug him, just because he was another human being and they were both alive. That was the miracle. But not wanting blood on his flying jacket, he confined himself to saying, "I'm glad you're alive."

"I wasn't planning to die," said the navigator, his voice pinched and nasal from his injury.

"We need to get away from the wreckage," said Mike. "People will have seen it going down."

People had, but only two men hunting in the nearby forest. They heard it first, and then, when they got closer, they saw the wreckage. They were hunting discreetly, because they could not be caught with a firearm, but they had to take the risk because food was scarce. It was not as bad in the eastern provinces as it was in the west, because food was still getting through. But there was not much.

The two men came to the edge of the forest and then stood still. They waited for the two airmen to see them, which they did after a couple of minutes. Then they beckoned to them.

Mike hesitated. "One of them is carrying a gun," he said.

"But they're not in uniform," said the navigator.

Mike made up his mind. "Let's risk it," he said. "Come on."

They began to walk over towards the hunters, who started to advance towards them. The one who had been carrying the gun had slung it over his shoulder.

"Americans?" he shouted.

"Yes," Mike shouted back. "American."

They approached each other gingerly. On seeing the blood on the navigator's face, one of the men reached into his pocket and passed him a handkerchief to press to his nose. Then the other one, who was fair-haired and taller than his companion, said, "You must come with us." He spoke slowly, but his English seemed good enough.

They looked at Peter Woodhouse in astonishment.

"Where did you find this dog?" the fair-haired man asked.

"He was with us," answered Mike. "Crew."

The fair-haired man translated this into Dutch, and his companion shook his head in mock disbelief.

"We were shot down," said Mike.

The man laughed. "I had worked that out," he said. Then he added, "Probably by the Germans." He laughed again. Then he turned serious, and indicated they should hurry.

"They'll be searching for you," he said. "We have to get you as far away from here as we can. Can you run, or at least walk faster than this?"

They set off. There was a path through the forest that they followed until they reached a narrow unpaved road. They did not follow this, but crossed it to reach another field in which again there was a track. Eventually they came to a farmyard; the man who spoke English said it was a friendly house.

"They will hide you," he said. "Then we'll get you away this evening." He looked at the navigator; he was clearly concerned. "We can find a doctor, if you like. Not today, but in a day or two. He could look at your nose."

'I think it's broken," said the navigator.

"I broke mine when I was a boy," said the man, pointing to the bridge of his nose. "See? It's not straight. But I can tell you something – women like a man with a broken nose."

He gestured to Peter Woodhouse. "We won't need to hide him. He can stay in the yard." Then he added, "Dogs are innocent, aren't they? This isn't their war."

The fair-haired man was called Mees; the other man was Pauel. It was Mees who did the talking when the farmer appeared. There was a low, murmured conversation in Dutch, accompanied by anxious looks in the direction of the two airman. The farmer pointed to Peter Woodhouse and asked a question; Mees shrugged and made a gesture of helplessness. Peter Woodhouse, who seemed completely unharmed by the crash landing, looked about him with interest, sniffing the farmyard scents.

The farmer came over to Mike, took his hand, and shook it.

"He says that there is a place in his barn where you will be safe," said Mees. "He says that we must try to get you out tonight, if possible. The Germans are everywhere in the area and they will be conducting searches once your plane is found."

Mike said that he understood. "We don't want to put anyone at risk."

Mees replied that they were used to risk; they had lived with it for four years, but now they could see the prospect of liberation and they could take a few more risks. "We're no longer on our own. The Canadians are not too far away. The Americans and the British too. It won't be too long now."

The farmer started to become concerned. He tapped his watch and then pointed at the barn. Mees said that they should go with the farmer; he would show them what to do, even if he could not tell them. He and Pauel would try to be back that night –"with people who can help you" – but they could not guarantee it.

They did come, though, just before midnight. Mees was there, but not Pauel, and there were two other men, who spoke no English and whose names weren't given. They took the two airmen from the barn and led them to a river bank. Peter Woodhouse was secured to a lead that Mees had brought, and he trotted along uncomplainingly beside Mike. On the edge of the river a small rowing boat was tied up beneath a spreading willow, and they were told to climb into it. The two unnamed men rowed; Mees sat in the stern, occasionally whispering something to the rowers.

An hour later they drew up where the river flowed into what seemed to be a small town. Bundled out of the boat, they were taken to a nearby house and led immediately upstairs and into a sparsely furnished attic. There were two rolls of bedding on the floor and a chair with a stub of candle. Peter Woodhouse was not taken upstairs, but was held in the kitchen by one of the men who had done the rowing. A few items of clothing had been left by the bedding, including a fresh shirt for the navigator, whose clothes had been stained with blood from his face; his nose had stopped bleeding by now.

"Your dog will be looked after by one of these people,"

explained Mees. "This is not the place for him."

They were left to go to bed. They used the candle for long enough to take off their flying boots and their jackets. They were both close to exhaustion, and Mike summoned just enough energy to blow out the candle before sleep claimed him.

The occupants of the house were an elderly man, Henrik, his son and daughter-in-law, and a ten-year-old boy named Dirk. Dirk brought them their evening meal on most days, and sometimes stayed until they had finished so he could take the plates away. He spoke no English, but occasionally addressed them in Dutch, apparently asking questions to which no answer could be given. Their diet was spartan: potatoes dressed with a thin meat or fish gruel; onions and cabbage; helpings of an oaten porridge that barely covered the bottom of the plate. They realised, though, that every scrap of this fare was taken from somebody else's table: the country was not far from starvation and the feeding of two extra mouths tested resources even further.

At least once a day Peter Woodhouse was brought up to spend half an hour or so with them in the attic. He seemed pleased to be reunited with them, wagging his tail and whining with pleasure in spite of the gloom of their attic hideaway. Mike could tell that the dog was losing weight, and he would save a scrap here and there from his own meagre rations to give to him when he came up.

Henrik, the owner of the house, took them downstairs to spend part of each morning in a small living room immediately below the attic. He spoke a few words of English and for the rest could make himself understood through an elaborate and idiosyncratic sign language. In this language, the Germans were signified by the puffing up of cheeks and the furrowing of the brow, to produce an impression of ire and menace.

They should keep away from the window, he indicated, although they could look out if they stood well back. Not that there was much to see, as the street outside was a quiet one. On several occasions, though, they saw a small German patrol – never more than five or six men – making its way down the street. They watched these passing men with fascination. These were the enemy, the cause of all this – their being in Europe in the first place, the danger they had been subjected to, their crash landing, their virtual imprisonment in an attic. And far away, of course, they knew far more serious things were happening, all brought about by these ordinary men in grey marching down the street of a small Dutch town, flesh and blood like them, no doubt with lives from which they themselves had been taken; yet the enemy, nonetheless.

Mees told them what was being done on their behalf. "It's too dangerous at the moment, but we'll try to get you back to your people. They aren't too far away now, and it may be safer just to keep you here until they arrive. We'll see."

Mike understood. "But every day we're here means more danger for these people." He gestured towards the floors below. "They would be shot if we were found."

Mees nodded. "Yes, but this is as safe as anywhere else – possibly safer. Those soldiers you may have seen out of the window stay just a few yards away, you know. They've taken over the school round the corner. They're your neighbours and it wouldn't occur to them that anybody's hiding a stone's throw away, under their own shadow." He smiled. "And anyway, Henrik looks after their building for them. Why would they search his house?"

Mike was incredulous. "He works for the Germans?"

Mees laughed. "What better cover?"

There was something else that was troubling both Mike and the navigator. It preyed on their minds that people might think them dead. They both knew what people at the base would have thought when their aircraft did not return: they themselves had thought exactly that of those who had not come back. *Missing in action: presumed dead.* The bleak conclusion was usually true, and that, surely, was what people would be thinking of them. Mike thought of Val and of what they would have said to her. He knew that they frowned on giving people false hope – that this only led to a postponement of grief. He concluded that there would have been little encouragement for her.

If only a message could somehow get through; not much of a message – just one word would do: *alive.* He asked Mees whether he could contact someone. "Just to tell them we're alive. A few words, that's all."

"We've done what we can," said Mees. "It's been our practice all along. But we're short of a wireless operator at the moment, and so we've used the Red Cross. We haven't been able to talk to them directly, but we've tried to send a message. They may have received it or they may not."

"And you have nothing for us? Nothing back?"

Mees shook his head sadly. "In these conditions, people often have to work in the dark. We work as cells – we've done that from the beginning. That means that information doesn't travel easily."

Mike felt that he had fallen into a world of darkness. There was the gloomy attic, with its tiny skylight that let in a shaft of light no wider than a man's hand; there was the room below, in which no lamp ever shone; there was the street onto which they were sometimes allowed to gaze, which was dark because of its narrowness; there was the whole continent that was plunged into such blackness at night because of curfews and blackouts and lack of streetlights. And alongside this all-embracing physical darkness there was a spiritual blanket that smothered all sense of joy and optimism. It was night, and although people talked of dawn, risked their lives to bring that moment forward, in so many places it was still the darkest of hours.

13

When Val asked for time off to go to the doctor the following day, Archie told her she could take the whole morning.

"Or, if you want, you can have the whole day," he said. "You deserve it. Not much going on round here."

That was not true. Val knew there was a long list of tasks that had to be done before the end of August, and that Archie was just trying to be kind to her. He had been over-solicitous ever since *that day*, which was the way she referred to the day of Mike's disappearance. She had eventually told him that she did not need special treatment, that there were plenty of people in the same position, and that she wanted to carry on doing her share irrespective of what had happened. She heard the expression *young widow* – there were plenty of those – and thought, *That is what I am*. But not quite: young widows had a status that she did not have; they were looked after with payments and pensions; they had their husband's name to hold on to; there was a whole world of officialdom to show support for them. She had none of that: she was just somebody who had lost her fiancé. People felt sorry for women in that position, but that was all there was to it. They thought *bad luck*, but then they went on to think of all the other things that engaged their sympathy, and for most that was a lengthy list.

"I don't need the whole day," she said. "I can see him in the morning. They said ten o'clock. Then I could get over here by twelve."

"If that's what you want." He paused, looking at her with undisguised curiosity. "You're not sickening for something?

This is hard work you're doing – I wouldn't want it to get to be too much."

She held his stare. "I can do the work," she said quietly.

She wished that he would leave it there, but he continued. "Because if you're sickening – after what happened, of course – nobody would blame you, you know. Folks know about what happened."

"Archie," she said patiently, "it's all right. There's nothing wrong with me."

He started to ask, "Then why . . ." but stopped himself. Women's problems, of course. *How stupid of me*, he thought. *Women have these problems, and I go and ask this poor girl.*

Blushing, he turned away. "I'll see you tomorrow," he said. "Whatever time you turn up."

The doctor's surgery was in a small town seven miles away from the village. There was a bus that left just before eight, but on a summer's morning it was no hardship to catch it after she had eaten breakfast with Annie and Willy.

"Why are you going to the doctor?" asked Willy. "You not well, or something?"

Annie looked at him. "Mind your own business, Willy," she said.

"A check-up," said Val. "You should go too, Willy. The doctor listens to your heart, and—"

"Nothing wrong with my heart," said Willy.

Val spread jam thickly on her toast. There would be no more butter for two days: they had used their ration and must do without, unless Willy could get hold of some from his new farm; he brought home milk and cream quite regularly. One of the other land girls worked on a dairy farm and was never short of butter; people said that she got it from the cowman in return for favours, but they always said things like that. She pointed a finger at Willy. "How do you know? There's something called a heart murmur, although you can't hear it yourself. The doctor listens . . ."

"Oh, I know all about that," said Willy. "He listens with one of them things . . ."

"Stethoscopes," said Annie. "And you'd better catch that bus, Val. Ten minutes."

They had told her to be there by eight-thirty, and the doctor would try to see her before nine. He was running late – a small boy had a bad cut on a finger that had to be stitched – but eventually she was taken in by the nurse, who sat in as chaperone. The nurse had a magazine with her, and read it discreetly in the corner until it was time for Val to be examined.

The doctor asked how long it was.

"Three weeks," she said.

The nurse looked up from her magazine, but dropped her eyes again.

"And you're usually regular?"

She nodded. "But I feel a bit different. I don't know how to put it, but I feel different. Sort of light."

The doctor was making a note. "Morning sickness usually starts about six weeks after you first miss," he said.

She could see the nurse looking at her. She wondered whether such people looked for a ring on the finger. Or did they take the view that it was none of their business – which it wasn't, in her view.

The doctor cleared his throat. "I'd like to examine you," he said. "But remember, it's too early to know with any certainty.

It'll become clear enough in time." He put the cap back on his pen, screwing it on with elaborate care while he asked the next question. "And the father?"

She felt the nurse's eyes boring into the back of her head. "I'm engaged," she said. "He's my fiancé."

The doctor relaxed. He glanced across the room at the nurse. "Well, that's not too bad, is it? The date of the wedding can be brought forward – if necessary." He allowed himself a smile.

Her heart was pounding. "But he's dead," she said. "The US Air Force. He flew a Mosquito." She had begun to come to terms with his death. Her earlier hope – slender at the best of times – had grown weaker with each day. She was beginning to mourn.

The doctor's face fell. "My dear young lady, I'm so sorry."

She looked down at the floor. She did not want to cry in front of these people, but it was hard. She had cried and cried so much that she thought she had used up what tears there were, yet it seemed there were still more to shed.

The nurse stood up. She crossed the room and put an arm about her shoulder. She had a small handkerchief in her hand, and offered this to her.

"All these brave young men," said the doctor. "We're losing all these brave young men. Our men. Americans. New Zealanders. Canadians. All of them." He shook his head. "And there doesn't seem to be an end to it."

The nurse spoke. "It'll come."

"Yes, nurse," said the doctor. "You may be right, but in the meantime, it still goes on." He rose to his feet. "I'll examine Miss Eliot now."

She had to wait more than an hour for a bus back to the

village. There was a small bus shelter, stale and dank, and she sat there thinking of what she would do. The doctor had said that there was a place they had used, a place near Cheltenham, that took girls in her position. "Not exactly the same position as yours," he said. "You're an engaged woman – or you were – which is almost the same as being married. Some of those girls don't have that advantage; some of them younger than you."

"Fifteen," said the nurse.

"Yes, fifteen. But they do what's necessary. They take them in and let them have the baby. Then the babies are placed."

She drew in her breath. "Placed?"

"For adoption," said the doctor. "There are other places, of course – some of them run by nuns. They look after you well, although some of the nuns, I believe, can be a bit on the severe side."

"Don't go to the nuns," said the nurse. "Stay away from them. You're not RC, are you? No, well, best to go somewhere else."

"The almoner at the hospital can help," said the doctor. "We have a very good woman there, Mrs Knight. She's probably the best person to advise you."

Now, sitting in the bus shelter, she imagined herself going off to one of those places. She would have to go early if people were not to notice. She could tell them she was going to another farm – somewhere further away – and that she would not be coming back for some time. Would she have to tell the Land Army people? They must know about these things, because she could not be the first land girl to be in this position. They may have their own place, for all she knew, where they sent girls who got themselves into trouble.

She would have to tell Annie – if she did not already know. No, she must know; she must. She had been able to work out what was going on and had said that it was all right with her. She had said that, hadn't she? She had said *it's different in wartime*, and she had been right. She probably knew that there was always a chance of this sort of thing happening. She must know that, being a postmistress and seeing all the things that postmistresses saw.

In the event, Annie did know. She had not said anything about Val's going to the doctor, because there would be only one reason why she needed to do that. A fit young woman like her – strong as an ox, with all that farm work – eating a good, healthy diet with those extra eggs and the milk that Willy brought back, cream sometimes; you would be healthy with all that and being nineteen too, twenty next month.

She called Annie out of the post office. There was nobody in at the time, and Annie came back to the kitchen to talk to her. "Well," she said. "Is everything all right?"

She did not answer immediately, and Annie came towards her. She took her in her arms. "Dearie, you know that I love you very much. If this is what has happened, it's because of the war – everything's because of the war." Annie paused. "What did he say? Did he say that you are?"

She nodded her head. "But he can't say definitely yet. He says I should go back in a few weeks."

Annie patted her gently, as one would a child. "Dearie, that's all right. I'll look after you – and the baby. You mustn't worry."

She told Annie about the almoner at the hospital, who was apparently the person to go to for advice. Annie shook her head. "That Mrs Knight is a gossip. I wouldn't tell her what time it was unless I didn't mind the whole world knowing. We'll find somebody else."

Val thought of something. "We'll have to tell Willy," she said. "Eventually. He'll . . . well, he'll see, won't he?"

"All in good time," said Annie. "No sense in getting Willy upset over anything just yet."

She considered this. 'No," she said. "I want to tell him earlier rather than later. It'll give him time to get used to it. You know how he is. He doesn't always understand things at first."

She started to cry, and Annie held her to her. Neither said anything for a few minutes. Then Annie said, "You're a good girl, Val. You've done everything right. You've worked hard. You made a good man happy. You've got nothing to be ashamed of – nothing at all."

14

He was a *Feldwebel*, a corporal, and was the second most senior soldier in the small unit posted in the town. The most senior was an *Oberfeldwebel*, a thin-faced man from Hamburg whom none of the men liked, and who was both lazy and unpredictable. The *Feldwebel* was called Karl Dietrich, but was known, for some reason, as Ubi. He was from Berlin and had recently turned twenty-two.

Ubi hated the war. He had joined up at seventeen under pressure from a threatening youth leader, who said he would denounce him for disloyalty if he failed to enlist. His father had tried to dissuade him, but he had been away when Ubi made the decision and on his return it was too late. He himself, a union leader, was already under suspicion and any suggestion that he had stopped his son from serving would have resulted in his arrest. Ubi had hated every moment of his training and had seriously considered desertion, but had been warned of the consequences by a close friend, a fellow infantryman, who had had the misfortune to have been detailed to serve in a firing squad.

The friend had said, "I'll never forget it. Never. I was sick over my rifle, over my boots, over everything."

His posting to Holland had saved him from being sent to the east, and once he was there the army seemed largely to have forgotten about him, to his great relief. He served in a number of small occupying garrisons, this last one being an ideal post for him because nothing much happened. There were regular searches, of course, and the occasional arrest. But for the most part they left the Dutch to get on with their lives provided they did nothing overt. They knew they were hiding people – all sorts of people, apparently – but in his view that was their business. The people they were hiding were small fry: undocumented foreigners, criminals on the run from somewhere, Jews. Ubi had nothing against Jews and could not understand the obsession of people like the *Oberfeldwebel*, who ranted about the bankers he said had brought Germany to her knees before their machinations had been exposed.

The only drawback to this posting, he felt, was the *Oberfeldwebel* himself. The locals were far too passive a bunch to do anything hostile, such as mount an ambush or blow something up; he rather liked them, with their slow, rather rustic ways and their guttural speech. He had even learned their language, since he had a good ear for these things, and it relieved the monotony to be able to talk to people in the street. If you spoke to them in Dutch, some of them could be quite friendly, although you always had those looks from others. The looks were hard to define: if they had been accompanied by a hostile gesture, then you could arrest the offender, but if they just looked it was harder to do anything about it.

"If anybody spits at you," advised the *Oberfeldwebel*, "bring him in. Spit is a weapon, especially in the mouth of a Dutchman. He'll regret it."

The *Oberfeldwebel*'s laziness at least meant that Ubi and his men were able to get on with their duties as they saw fit, which was with a lack of enthusiasm and a discretion that ensured they encountered little trouble. They made sure that their patrols were on the periphery of their allotted territory, so that neighbouring commanders should see them and assume a high level of activity on their part. This worked, and no attempts were made to relocate them to more hazardous posts. With any luck, Ubi thought, they might spend the rest of the war exactly where they were. How the war would end was something he did not care to dwell upon: when first he joined up he had assumed the invincibility of Germany; then had come North Africa and Italy and now the landings in Normandy. Germany would make peace, he hoped, and everyone could go home honourably; or, and this he feared was more likely, they would be hounded and pursued to the end. That man was mad, with all his ranting and raving, and his disastrous foray into the mud and snow of the Ukraine; he would carry on with his delusions until the Russians and Americans overran him and Germany ceased to exist. He dreamed of Russian soldiers – vague, shadowy figures who looked at him from encircling darkness and then slipped away, vanished, when he tried to confront them. In his dreams, death came as a wakening up, and he found himself coming to, sweating and uncomfortable, in his shared room with the shape of the two other men under their blankets a few feet away, enduring, for all he knew, their own nocturnal demons.

Ubi had got to know Henrik, who was in their building several times a day, attending to blocked drains and matters of that sort. He was paid for two hours of work a day, but he seemed to spend more time than that there, which suited the men as he would also make coffee, bake bread, and keep the kitchen neat and tidy for the *Oberfeldwebel* who, in spite of his laziness, was particular about cleanliness.

When Ubi called at Henrik's house eight days after the arrival of Mike and the navigator, Henrik assumed that the visit had something to do with his duties at the garrison building. He had started to paint one of the barrack rooms, as the Germans had somehow got hold of several tins of paint – stolen them, he imagined – and he had started but not finished the job the previous day.

Henrik knew that the two airmen were in the attic and that they were careful about making no noise, and so he was not too concerned. But then he remembered something: Peter Woodhouse was sleeping on the mat in front of the kitchen range and it was into the kitchen that he had invited Ubi.

It was too late to do anything – Ubi had seen the dog.

"So, Henrik, you have a dog. You never told me that."

Henrik tried to smile. "Oh, that dog. He belongs to a friend . . . a friend who's ill and can't look after him."

Ubi nodded. "That's why it's useful to have friends," he said. "They can help you out when you're in a spot."

"Very true," said Henrik. "Keep your friends happy – you never know when you'll need them."

Ubi crossed the room to stand over Peter Woodhouse. Then he bent down to stroke the dog's coat. "He looks a bit thin," he said. "But then I suppose these are hard times for dogs as well as people."

"He likes fish," said Henrik hurriedly. "I catch fish for him from time to time. It's fine, as long as I take all the bones out."

"Bones," said Ubi. "Have you ever tried eating pike? Those bones they have! Like arrowheads."

"Good flesh, though," said Henrik. He was watching Ubi as he stroked Peter Woodhouse. He saw the collar, and he turned cold inside. The collar: the most basic mistake imaginable, and they had made it. With all their care, with all their insistence on anonymity and silence and doing things by night – in spite of all that, they had forgotten his collar.

Ubi was looking at the collar now, squinting to read the words burned into the leather. This, thought Henrik, is how death comes: through a little thing, in slow motion, while people are having dinner and walking in the street and the wildfowl on the river are drifting with the stream; this is how death comes.

Ubi read the name. "Peter Woodhouse," he said. "How do you people spell Peter, Henrik? Isn't it with an i – *Pieter*?"

He twisted the collar round so that he could see the rest of the inscription. At first he said nothing, then he said, "An American dog! Well, that's unusual, isn't it?"

Henrik had been thinking. "Oh, somebody gave that collar to my friend. He got hold of it in Amsterdam. It must be a leftover from something – heaven knows what. But it fits him, and so we've left it on."

Ubi was looking at him with a strange expression. Henrik swallowed. If he were handed over to the Gestapo, would he be able to bear the torture? He doubted it: younger, stronger men than he gave in, within minutes sometimes. Anything to end the pain, they said.

Ubi came back across the room so that he was now standing close to Henrik.

"I believe I should search your house, Henrik," he said. "We haven't searched you yet, have we?"

Henrik shook his head mutely.

"And why should we?" continued Ubi. "What need is there to search our friends?"

Henrik said nothing. He saw that Ubi had his pistol on his belt. He could hit him over the head or push him down the stairs or something, he thought; but no, he could not. Ubi was well built and would overpower him effortlessly, even without having to shoot him.

"Shall we go upstairs?" asked Ubi. "There's obviously nothing down here – apart from our friend over there."

He had no alternative but to accompany Ubi up the stairs. He waited while Ubi looked in the three rooms on the floor above, opening cupboards and glancing under beds.

"I'm sure I'll find nothing," Ubi said. "This is just a formality, Henrik."

He looked up at the ceiling. He noticed the small stepladder left against the wall.

"An attic?" he asked.

"Yes," said Henrik, raising his voice. "An attic."

Ubi frowned. "Why so loud, Henrik?" He looked up at the ceiling. Then he fixed Henrik with a stare. *He knows. He knows.*

Ubi pointed to the trapdoor. Then he leaned close to Henrik and whispered, "Guests, Henrik?"

Henrik froze. He opened his mouth to say something, but he could not find the breath, or the words.

Ubi continued to whisper. "Listen very carefully, Henrik, my friend. I can do one of two things: I can fire my pistol through the window, which will alert the garrison and they'll be here in less than a minute, or – and this is what I'd much prefer – you invite your guests to come down and say hello in the proper manner." He paused. "That keeps all this just between ourselves."

Henrik made his decision. Reaching for the stepladder, he placed it underneath the trapdoor and climbed its few steps to the top. Then he pushed the trapdoor open and called out in his limited English, "Come, now."

They complied.

Ubi looked at the two men standing before him. He had

drawn his pistol, and they were looking at it nervously. He turned to Henrik and asked him who the men were.

"American airmen," said Henrik. The blame must be his alone: he must try to convince them of that, then only one person would die. "My family doesn't know about them – just me."

Ubi smiled. "Oh yes? Well, of course not. I don't suppose they speak Dutch or German, do they?"

"No," said Henrik.

"Pity," said Ubi, replacing his pistol in its holster. "Because I would like to ask them if I could bring them some food. They must be hungry."

Henrik stared at the soldier. "You'd do that?" he stuttered, his voice breaking with emotion.

"Yes, I would." He shrugged. "How much longer is this war going to go on? One month? Six months? Who can tell, but why should more men die?" He looked down at Henrik with what appeared to be fondness. "We're not going to win, yet if I took these men in we would shoot you and your son, and your daughter-in-law, and who wants that?"

Henrik said nothing. Then he turned to Mike and pointed at Ubi. Then he pointed at his own heart, twice, and placed his finger against his lips. It was the only way he could think of saying what he could not say.

He waited to see if they understood. They did. Mike reached forward, offering a hand to Ubi, who shook it, smiling as he did so.

Ubi said to Henrik, "Nobody knows about this, Henrik. Understand?"

Henrik nodded. "Except God," he said.

15

Val spoke to Willy the day after her visit to the doctor's surgery. It was in the evening, and the two of them were alone in the house, Annie having gone out for a meeting of her wool group. They unravelled old woollen garments, rolling up the wool for re-use, and exchanged news as they did so. It was, Val had suggested, the clearing house for local gossip – and now, she realised, she would be of prime interest in that respect: talked about, disapproved of, the moment her aunt left the circle.

Willy was doing the washing up when she spoke to him. He liked to scrub the pots energetically, priding himself on making them gleam.

"I've something to tell you, Willy," she began.

He continued with his task. "This one's getting old. Metal's thin."

"That's because you scrub it too hard." She paused. "Are you listening to me, Willy? It's something important."

"I can listen and do this at the same time."

She waited a moment. "I'm going to have a baby."

He laid the pot down on the sink and turned to face her. "You? You're going to have a baby?"

"Yes," she said. "Not for some time yet, and the doctor hasn't said definitely. But I think so."

She heard his breath coming in short spurts. "Why?" His voice was strained.

"Well, I just am. I'm going to have a baby."

His eyes were wide. "But you're not married."

"No, but you can still have babies if you're not married."

This took a little while to sink in. "I know about all that," he said. "You been doing all that with him? Even you?"

She lowered her eyes. "Even me, Willy. Yes. Since you ask."

"And now he's dead," muttered Willy. "So what are people going to say?"

She was prepared for this. Willy, for all his innocence, was acutely aware of what people might say. That came, she imagined, from having been laughed at by others; you became sensitive to their sneers. "I don't care what people say." She did, of course.

Willy sat down. "But you can't have people talking about you. You can't have that. Talking. Laughing. Pointing their finger and saying *she's got no husband, but there's a baby, you know.* You can't have that."

"People always talk, Willy. You have to live with it. Let them talk." She paused, the old rhyme from childhood returning – the playground mantra of the bullied: *Sticks and stones may break my bones but words will never hurt me.* She recited it now to Willy.

"Words can hurt," he said. "They can."

"Well, there's far worse things going on," she said.

He became silent. She watched him, the mental effort of whatever he was thinking about writ large on his face.

"I could marry you," he said at last. "I'll marry you and then it'll be all right."

She held him in her gaze. She realised that he meant it; that this was no idle offer, this was a proposal.

"But Willy . . ."

"Cousins can marry. Lots of cousins marry."

She shook her head. "Not lots, Willy. Sometimes maybe . . .

And anyway, we aren't proper cousins. We're what they call *connected* . . ."

"And there ain't nothing wrong with it. You can have a proper church wedding and all."

"Oh, Willy . . ."

"And it would mean that I'd be your baby's dad. A baby needs a dad. He needs somebody to help him."

She knew she had to stop him before he went any further.

She looked for a reason that he would understand. "I can't marry you, Willy. I can't do that because you marry people you love – and we aren't in love, are we? I like you, I like you very much, but you aren't in love with me and I'm not in love with you. That means we can't get married."

He said nothing.

She spoke hurriedly, putting the matter beyond further discussion. "So while I'm really grateful to you for the offer – and it's a kind idea, really it is – we just can't get married." She paused. "So, soon enough I'll make up my mind about what I'm going to do – I'll probably go away somewhere – and then I'll tell you. You can come and visit me."

It worked. He smiled at the invitation to visit. "And bring things for your baby?"

"Of course," she said. "And if it's a boy, he'll want to spend a lot of time with you."

He beamed with pleasure. "I can teach him things," he said. "Since he won't have a dad, I can do that."

"Of course you can, Willy."

She left the room so that he should not see her tears. She went outside, into the darkness. Here and there a chink of light escaped the blackout curtains, but otherwise there was nothing.

A dog barked somewhere, and she found herself thinking of Peter Woodhouse and how he had been caught up in the madness of war – a necessary madness, as somebody had put it. She looked up into the sky and wondered how her desperate willing that Mike should be alive could make any difference in a world as large and indifferent as this one was. The answer, of course, was that it could not, and that no amount of hope and prayer had the slightest impact. There was no justice, no fairness; there was nothing that would guarantee that we rather than they won. There was just chance, and death, and the emptiness that death brought.

She went back inside. Willy had finished his work on the pot and was looking about for something else to polish or put away. She crossed the room to him and planted a kiss on his cheek. "I'm so proud of you," she said.

He blushed. "Can't think why," he said.

16

News came through Mees, who listened to the BBC and *Radio Oranje* regularly. He was optimistic, and his optimism buoyed their mood. "It won't be long now. The British are very close to Eindhoven," he said. "That's not far away. We'll be able to hand you over."

"And the Canadians?" asked Mike.

"Not far away either."

"It's hard being cooped up here. I'm sorry, but it's hard."

Mees understood. "There's no point trying to pass you down the line," he pointed out. "You're safe here. Our friend helps."

Our friend was his name for Ubi. He liked him less than Henrik did. "Can you trust a German?" he had asked.

"Yes," came Henrik's reply. "The Germans do what they say they're going to do. And besides, he's taking as much risk as we are. He's also looking down the barrel of a gun if he's found out."

In September they heard artillery in the distance, and when Ubi came to see them, as he did every day, he said there were rumours that Nijmegen had been taken. Mees said to him, "Do you want to desert? We'll shelter you, you know."

He thought about it, but at last said that he would not. The *Oberfeldwebel* would step up searches if he did, as a traitor was an irresistible quarry. He would be keener to find him than he was to ferret out Resistance people; it would just create trouble.

"When the time comes, I'll give myself up," he said.

That month, Eindhoven was liberated. "They're fifteen miles away," said Mees. "We can start counting the days."

In the garrison, the duties remained much the same. They did patrols; they logged entries in their book of buildings searched. They came across a small cache of arms in a house near the canal. They set fire to the house, its occupants having fled, and lifted the two pigs they found in the back yard and took them back to the garrison in a handcart. One of the men had been a butcher, and he did the slaughtering, being badly bitten in the leg by one of his victims in the process. Ubi watched, sickened by the sight. More blood, he thought. Pig's blood, human blood. Blood.

Some of the men talked openly about the end of the war. One had been listening to a clandestine broadcast that spoke of the Russians' progress. There was talk of the rape that would follow. Ubi thought of his mother and his sister. He wondered whether they could flee west, where the Americans might hold the Red Army in check.

The *Oberfeldwebel* gave the occasional pep-talk. He told the men that every great victory was preceded by set-backs. There was a secret weapon that would make the V2 rockets look tame. It was not long before it would be unveiled and then Churchill and Stalin would change their tune. In the meantime, they had their work to do and they would do it.

One morning the *Oberfeldwebel* decided that it was time to make a show of force. The entire unit – all twelve men – would accompany him and the *Feldwebel* on a march around the town. This would show any elements of the population who thought they might be giving up that they were still very much in control.

As they made their way down the main street, they encountered Mees, who was walking Peter Woodhouse, no longer wearing his compromising collar but being led on the end of a string with a makeshift noose. The dog became tense as the sound of marching approached. When the men drew level with him, he growled and began to bark. Mees struck him on the back with the rolled-up newspaper he was carrying, but this had no effect. The barking became hysterical. Mees looked as apologetic as he could, because he saw the Germans looking in his direction, and tugged at the string lead. Enraged, Peter Woodhouse slipped out of his collar.

There was nothing Mees could do other than shout and run after him. But it was too late: Peter Woodhouse had reached the first of the Germans and had lunged at the boots of one of the men. The soldier kicked out at him and Peter Woodhouse attacked again.

It was Ubi who managed to get him under control. Surprised by the familiar smell of someone whom he had by now got to know, Peter Woodhouse calmed down and began to lick his friend's hand. The *Oberfeldwebel* shouted an order and another of the men stepped forward, loosened his belt, and put it round Peter Woodhouse's neck.

"Dietrich," shouted the *Oberfeldwebel*. "Take that dog round the corner and shoot him."

Ubi frowned. "He's just a dog," he muttered. "Can't we just . . ."

He was not allowed to finish. A small group of children had gathered, and the *Oberfeldwebel* gestured towards them. The locals might need to be taught a lesson from time to time, but shooting a dog in front of children was unnecessary.

Ubi tried to dissuade the *Oberfeldwebel*, but his pleas had no effect. "You've been given an order," came the response. "Carry it out unless you want to face the consequences."

He stood for a few moments while Mees approached the *Oberfeldwebel*, begging him to excuse the dog. "He meant no harm," he said. "He was over-excited, that's all."

The *Oberfeldwebel* signalled him away with a movement of his pistol. "I will not have my men attacked by dogs," he said. "Consider yourself fortunate that you are not being placed under arrest yourself."

Mees knew that he must not be arrested. He knew far too much about what people in the area were doing to subvert the occupation to allow himself to be handed over to the Gestapo. He could not run the risk of compromising those whose identity he knew. He made a gesture of acceptance and moved off.

Ubi began to lead Peter Woodhouse away. The men were told that they could break for a smoke, and they did so, sitting on the edge of the town fountain, lighting up and talking among themselves. Round the corner, in the small deserted alley that led off the main street, Ubi dragged Peter Woodhouse into the doorway of a now closed tobacconist shop. The dog looked up at him and tried to lick his hand again. Ubi drew his pistol.

He pulled the trigger, the shot reverberating against the walls of the houses in the narrow street. The bullet, aimed up in the air, sped harmlessly away.

Peter Woodhouse cowered. "Go," hissed Ubi, aiming a kick at the dog's rump. "Run."

At first Peter Woodhouse simply continued to cower, but then a second kick, sharper than the first, made him move away. Ubi reached down to pick up a small stone at the edge of the road. He threw this at the dog as hard as he could and it connected with his snout, making him yelp. Slowly he began to move away, and then he broke into a faster run when Ubi sent another stone rattling down the street.

A week later, they heard the sound of tanks, an unmistakable low growl coming from the south. There was some gunfire, but that did not last long, and the sound of the approaching tanks grew much louder. At three o'clock the following afternoon, a tank drew up at the bridge on the edge of the town, allowing a platoon of infantry to run down the road, dropping for cover from time to time as they tested the town's defences. A few shots were fired from the direction of the garrison, and these drew a fusillade of machine gun fire from two separate positions. A white flag cloth quickly appeared at one of the garrison windows – a towel, it seemed – and this was waved energetically until a small line of men came out of the front door, their hands raised high in surrender. Almost immediately the bell in the church began to toll and people appeared in the streets. Dutch flags, hidden in anticipation of this day, were waved by excited children.

Mees ran to the house where Mike and the navigator were hiding. He led them out into the street and urged them on to the main square. They blinked at the light. A woman threw her arms around Mike and kissed him. The navigator looked stunned, and kept glancing up at the sky, as if expecting imminent attack.

They watched as the Germans were given their instructions. Two Allied soldiers kept guard over them, occasionally prodding them with the butts of their rifles and kicking in their direction. An officer appeared and reprimanded the men; then he spoke to the *Oberfeldwebel* in pidgin German. Mees came up and drew the officer aside, telling him that one of the garrison had collaborated with the Resistance.

"Don't point him out to me," said the officer. "They'll kill him."

"I can give you his name," said Mees. "He deserves consideration."

The officer nodded, and wrote it down in his notebook. The *Oberfeldwebel* watched.

Mike and the navigator did not know what to do. They spoke to the officer after he had finished with the *Oberfeldwebel*. He said, "Don't do anything just now. We'll ask somebody to come and fetch you. It's all a bit mixed up at the moment, but the situation will become clearer in due course." He looked at the two airmen. "Is there anything I can do for you in the meantime? Need anything?"

Mike nodded. "Could you send a message to our unit?. They don't know we're alive."

The officer nodded. 'Write the details down. I'll try to get it sent from Eindhoven."

One of Mees's friends appeared with Peter Woodhouse. The officer frowned. "What's this?"

Mike smiled as he explained. "Our dog. Our unit's mascot. He was shot down with us."

The officer looked astonished. "He was in the plane?"

"Yes," said Mike. He noticed that the *Oberfeldwebel* was staring at the dog. "Sir, you must take one of those men into protective custody."

The officer looked irritated. "Why?" He indicated Mees. "This man's already spoken to me about him."

"No, you must." Mike's voice had a note of urgency in it.

The officer bristled. He was a captain, and a senior one at that, but he was not sure if he outranked this scruffy aviator. "I'm not sure you can tell me what to do."

Mike fixed him with a cold stare. "I'm a serving officer. I'll take him as my prisoner."

The officer's lip curled. "He's under my custody."

Mees said, "I'll take him. He can be a prisoner of the Resistance."

The officer shook his head. "Don't be ridiculous. I don't know who you are." He hesitated. He had seen the *Oberfeldwebel* looking at Ubi, and he understood. Stepping forward, he pointed at Ubi. "You – you there. You come with me."

Mees quickly translated the command. His relief was palpable.

Ubi stepped forward. He looked at Mike and smiled. Then he bent down and patted Peter Woodhouse gently on the back. "War's over," he murmured.

The dog looked up at him. He was not sure: this was the man who had kicked him and thrown stones at him. The canine memory for that sort of thing is a long one. But something told him that all that was over. He had no word for it, but dogs can forgive, and he did.

17

Val asked Willy to peel the potatoes for their dinner that night. She had three large eggs, given to her by Archie. She had told him that she did not feel entitled to them, as he had already given her two that week, but he insisted. She was going to make egg and potato pie – a dish that she knew both Willy and Annie particularly liked. The white sauce would have to be made without butter, but the richness of the eggs would make up for that.

It had not been a good day. She had felt unwell early in the morning, which might have been morning sickness, she thought, or might have been something unconnected with the pregnancy. She had examined herself in the full-length mirror on the outside of her wardrobe, standing naked, sideways and then full on, to see whether her body was changing shape. She thought it was, although how big would the baby be at this stage? Tiny, she decided. The size of a mouse, perhaps, tucked away in her stomach somewhere vaguely down there: precise female anatomy had never been properly explained at school, although the girls had been taken aside for instruction and a visiting nurse had shown them a coloured diagram that none of them had properly understood. It was all tubes, she thought, and the baby was somewhere at the end of one of them, in the womb, wherever that was. She relaxed her muscles and her belly sagged – more so than normal, she thought. So she was beginning to show, she told herself: people would be able to tell in a month, perhaps a little longer.

She looked at her bust. She had never been proud of it

because she thought it was too schoolgirlish, too small. She had seen the women painted on the front of the American planes at the base – some of them completely naked, others wearing very little, and they all had much larger busts. They held them out before them like those carvings seamen had on the prow of sailing ships; that's what men liked, it seemed: women with that sort of bust, not one like hers. And yet Mike had said that her body was "just perfect", and she thought he had meant it.

Now he would never see her like this. He would never see her carrying his child. He would never be able to put his hand on her stomach and feel the baby move within, which is what she had been told fathers-to-be liked to do – to feel the life they had helped to create. That would not happen.

A few days earlier she had been able to tell herself that she might see him again. She had felt that if she gave up all hope for him, she would somehow be bringing about his death. It was a superstitious belief: talk of a man dying and you make it happen. People said something like that; she had heard them. So you didn't speculate as to somebody's chances, or at least not openly.

But then she started to admit to herself that the possibility of his survival was, as they had told her, extremely slender. And what had made it worse was that the day before, when she had delivered eggs to the base, Sergeant Lisowski had asked her whether she wanted any of Mike's things. He had been as tactful as he could, saying that she could just "look after" them and give them back if he ever returned, but she knew that what was happening was a disposal of his effects. There was not much, he said: some personal family photographs that would go back to his family in Muncie, along with his diary and an inscribed wristwatch that had his father's initials on it. But there were some other things – small things – that they would not normally send all the way back to the States and she might like as mementos.

She had said she would like them, and he had gone off to fetch a linen drawstring bag. He had given it to her without opening it to show her the contents, and it was not until she had returned to the house that she went to her room and opened the neck of the bag.

There was a penknife. There was a set of navigator's calipers; there was a bow tie with red and blue stripes. There was the framed picture he had taken of her. She laid these things out on the bed and then knelt at the side and let her head rest on the quilt. She reached for the bow tie, put it to her lips and kissed it. She wiped her eyes with the back of her hand. She muttered "Mike" and then "My love, my love", and she repeated these words over and over again, her tears making the bedcover moist, their salt in her mouth.

Now, as Willy peeled the potatoes for the egg and potato pie, she stood in the doorway and stared at his back. Should she have let Willy marry her? There would have been raised eyebrows, as many people would think that a woman should not take up with a man who was not quite all there. It was as if doing that would be to take advantage of him in some undefined way – sexual, perhaps. But he would be loyal, and kind, because both of these qualities were in his nature, and he would not make her unhappy.

But then she told herself that what she had said to him – even if it was intended to be a simple explanation readily understood by somebody like him – was, in fact, the right thing to say. She believed that you married for love – you had to if you wanted it to work. She knew that there were women who married for money or for land, but were they truly married in the real sense of the word? Or were they just signing up for a business arrangement in which they gave what women gave their husbands in return for a roof over their heads and the necessities of life? It was possible that Willy would find somebody who would actually love him, and he needed to have that chance. There could well be a girl somewhere, a farmer's daughter maybe, who would be right for him. She would be plain, perhaps, but strong and resourceful. She would cook and darn clothes and keep the kitchen range well stoked up. And if she were a farmer's daughter and there were no sons, then Willy could succeed to a farm and have his own place. That was possible, just possible.

Willy finished peeling the potatoes. He turned to Val and said, "All done. Good potatoes too. None of those black things in them – what do you call those black things, Val?"

"Eyes," she said.

He smiled. "That's right – eyes. No eyes."

She crossed the room to stand beside him. The eggs were in a brown paper bag, and she reached into this to extract one of them. "Look at this," she said. "I think I know which hen laid this one. She's a Rhode Island Red and she's bigger than the others."

He took the egg from her gingerly. "Shall I put it in the pan?"

"Yes, and then we'll put the other ones in with it and fill it with water. They need to be hard-boiled for our pie."

He said, "That's six minutes at least."

She nodded, and remembered that Willy had difficulty

telling the time. She had tried to teach him when she realised this, but he had struggled to master the concept of minutes to the hour. Why, he asked, if you counted up to thirty up to the figure six, did you then start counting down? Her explanation, she feared, had been less than clear and had merely added to his confusion.

They put the egg pan on the stove and switched it on. It was an unsophisticated electric cooker, and it took a long time to get to temperature. But they were lucky; plenty of people had nothing so advanced, and relied on ranges fuelled by wood or coal.

Willy was looking out of the window. "That sergeant fellow," he said. "Did you invite him?"

She frowned. "No. Is he outside?"

"He's coming by here," said Willy. "Maybe he wants more eggs."

She moved to the window and looked out. Sergeant Lisowski was making his way down the front path – and he had a dog with him.

"He's got hold of another dog," said Willy. "He must have been missing Peter Woodhouse." He turned to Val. "Ain't that nice, Val? Him getting another dog like that."

She did not answer. Making her way to the front door, she took a deep breath, brushed her hair back from her forehead, and opened to the sergeant's knock.

Peter Woodhouse leapt up at her. It was a headlong dive, and she reeled under the onslaught. She almost fell over, but righted herself as the dog managed to lick her face, covering her with dog spittle. He was whimpering, the sort of excited whimpering that comes when a dog is overcome with emotion.

Sergeant Lisowski stood there beaming. "He remembers you," he said. 'He hasn't forgotten."

"Is it really him?" she stuttered.

"Yes," said Sergeant Lisowski. "It's Peter Woodhouse. Look at the collar."

She struggled to get a sight of the collar. There was so much fur, so much wriggling dog muscle, that it was difficult to see the inscription. But it was there.

And then the full significance of this hit her, and she let out a scream.

"He's alive," said Sergeant Lisowski. "He'll be back in two or three days."

She screamed again. Willy was there now, and he was struggling to understand what was happening.

"Mike made it," said Sergeant Lisowski. "They sent the dog first because he didn't need a seat. Mike's waiting for a plane that's going out there soon. It'll bring him back."

Val flung her arms around the sergeant. He smelled of cooking, she thought, because he spent his days in the cookhouse. She kissed him on his neck, his chin, his cheek. He kissed her back and said, "I shouldn't kiss another fellow's girl, but what the heck."

They told Val that she could see him the day after his return. The colonel, who had returned from London, saw Mike while Val waited outside the office. It was the day after VE Day, when the formal capitulation of Germany had occurred, and there were still signs of the previous day's celebrations. Somebody had tied a balloon to a fire bucket, and it was still there, half deflated.

"Well, it's over," said the colonel. "At least, this bit of it." He paused. "And I think I know what you want to talk to me about."

Mike told him that they wanted to marry as soon as possible and would like his permission. The colonel suppressed a sigh. These wartime marriages were troublesome; he had seen many of them come unstuck once the glamour faded – as it did. He gave his permission. And then he said that Peter Woodhouse, US Air Force, Dog First Class could be officially reinstated as a mascot, if that was all right with the people who owned him, but was not to fly without permission. Mike thanked the colonel, and said that he felt one forced landing was enough for any dog.

The colonel laughed. "And your own future?" he said. "I've heard that you might want to stay in. Is that correct?"

Mike nodded. "I like flying, sir. It's what I want to do with my life." When he had entered the air force, he had had only a vague interest in flying. Now that had all changed, and he had discovered it was the thing that he wanted to do above all else.

He tried to explain it to the colonel. "When I'm up there, sir, up above the clouds, I just feel . . . well, I feel that I'm in the right place – for me, that is. That's where I have to be."

The colonel smiled. There was no need for that feeling to be explained to him; he knew. "Uncle Sam will still need pilots. And I think I can recommend you."

It was a strange moment for Mike. He had committed himself to a career, and he had chosen the woman he wanted to marry. It seemed to him as if the contours of his life, which had always been uncertain, were now set out as clearly and firmly as the lines on any map.

Willy gave Val away, leading her down the aisle of the small church not far from the post office. She was visibly pregnant by the time of the wedding, but people pretended not to notice. Archie, uncomfortable in an unaccustomed suit, sang the hymns loudly and out of tune. Afterwards, they went to the pub, where the landlord had laid out some of the tinned food that Mike had purloined from Sergeant Lisowski.

He had told her that their future would still be uncertain. There was still work for the air force to do in Europe – they had been warned that this would not finish any time soon – and he hoped she would not mind if they did not make it to Muncie, Indiana just yet. She said that she could accept that, as long as they went there sometime.

The honeymoon was the last three days of the leave the colonel had granted Mike. They travelled in a borrowed car, using American fuel, to a small port in Cornwall and climbed on the cliffs. They looked out in the direction of France, far away at that point, and were both for a moment silent with their thoughts.

A breeze came up off the sea. She asked, inconsequentially, "What are you thinking of?'

He turned to look at her. "I guess I was thinking of Peter Woodhouse."

She smiled. She had no idea why she should have been thinking of Peter Woodhouse just then, but she was.

"So was I," she said.

He smiled. "Do you think that it happens?"

"What happens?"

"Synchronicity."

She looked puzzled. He was studying engineering – or had been – and that made him a scientist, she supposed; she knew nothing of science, and the words that went with it.

He explained. "It's what happens when people start doing things – or thinking things – at the same time." He paused. "They say that it happens a lot with married couples." He blushed – neither of them was used to the fact of marriage. In the bed and breakfast in which they were staying, he had spoken the words "my wife" with such hesitation and awkwardness as to attract a look of doubt to the owner's face. Mike had intercepted the glance to the hand, and to the rings – that had allayed suspicion, but the fact still seemed strange to him. How did married people behave? Was he convincing as a married man?

Val liked the idea. "I wouldn't have to ask you to do things," she said. "I'd just have to think them."

"And I'd do what you wanted," said Mike.

"Exactly."

They spent a great deal of their time talking about the future. She seemed to have an insatiable appetite for information about Muncie and Indianapolis. What colour would the roof be? It would be red – he had no hesitation in answering that. And the kitchen? It would have everything, he promised, including a refrigerator large enough to walk into – well, almost – and cupboards with sliding doors.

And she asked what they would do.

He frowned. "Do?"

"Yes, what would we do . . . with our time?"

He looked thoughtful. "Go for drives in the car. Have you heard of drive-in movie theatres?"

She had not, and he explained. "They're going to be big. Every town's getting one now. You park your car, you see, and you watch the movie from the car. Twenty-five cents a person, and they sell hot dogs, popcorn . . . everything."

"I'd like that."

"Of course you would. We'd go every week – maybe twice a week."

"America," she sighed. It seemed an impossible dream: safety, refrigerators, drive-in movies. If only the war would end, with them alive when it did. She closed her eyes and thought that if that happened, then she might stop doubting that God existed and say yes, of course he does, because he would have brought them through this. It was almost a challenge to him, if he was there: prove it to me.

Suddenly an idea occurred to her. "Do people believe in God in Muncie?" she asked.

He looked surprised. "But of course they do," he answered.

"All of them?"

"Pretty much." Then he said, "And here? Don't people believe here?"

She thought for a moment. "They say they do, but I'm not so sure that they do – underneath. Maybe they *hope* that he's there."

"It's easier if you believe," he said. "It makes you feel a bit . . ." He trailed off.

Braver, she thought. *It makes you feel braver.*

"It makes you feel braver?"

He smiled. "Boy, do we need that."

It was the closest he came to telling her how frightened he was, but she understood, and she steered the conversation

away, onto something less real. She asked about drive-in movie
theatres, and about where the sound came from. Did you leave
your windows open?

He smiled at her. "You'll see," he said.

TWO

HE HATED THE WAR

18

A small square of roughly cut brown bread, stale and heavy, with a mug of lumpy soup scraped out of an urn. No meat in the soup, but a rancid smell that could have come from meat, an unfortunate horse, perhaps, or ancient pig; a thin layer of grease, too, across the surface that suggested the same origins.

Ubi took it gratefully, warming his hands on the mug, which was made of tin and conducted heat well. It was early May, and the air was far from warm, even if the hedges were green once more and there were wildflowers everywhere, and early blossom on the fruit trees. The man next to him spilled some of his soup down his chin and onto the jacket of his uniform; his hands were shaking and it was hard for him to bring the mug to his lips. He looked sheepishly at Ubi, who smiled at him encouragingly. There were many who seemed to be fumbling or faltering in unexpected ways – tripping, or stumbling, as if some internal gyroscope had been taken from them. One man, a *Feldwebel* like Ubi, seemed to have lost control of his bladder and sat dejectedly and self-consciously separate from the other men, staring up at the sky as if he were somewhere else, as if this were not him, this reeking, shameful person, a disgrace to the uniform he had so thoroughly ruined. Ubi took him an extra piece of bread that he found near the table where the rations had been handed out, and gave it to him in a gesture of support. The man took it, and looked up at him, briefly, but then looked away again without thanking him.

It was the midday meal. There would be something more at six o'clock, they had been told, although it might not be warm. One of their Canadian captors, a sergeant with a loud voice, had explained – through an interpreter – that they could not expect much more because their own people had robbed the Netherlands of most of its food. "So you see what this brings you," he announced. "What goes round, comes round. Understand?" He looked again at the puzzled faces and repeated his question. "Understand?"

Because of the intervention of Mees and the captain who had taken their surrender, Ubi had been put into a different prisoner-of-war holding centre from the rest of his unit. The captain had decided that if this were done there would be little risk of retaliation from his former superiors or his colleagues – the chances of their encountering him among the thousands of prisoners of war caught up behind the rapidly advancing Allied lines would be next to non-existent. A note was left with the senior Canadian officer at the makeshift detention camp to the effect that *Feldwebel* Dietrich was alleged to have been helpful to the Resistance and to a group of American airmen. This could be entered on his records, although nobody was sure what records there would be and who would hold them. At the camp itself, there was the barest noting down of name, age and unit, with nothing said about anything else.

On the third day of his captivity, when they were still bedding down in a field, all two hundred of them, watched over by sentries posted along an ordinary stock fence, the Canadian officer in charge insisted on an examination of every prisoner. In the raw spring air they took off their tunics and their shirts, and lined up in front of a couple of non-commissioned officers. Each man then held out his left arm to be checked for an SS number tattooed on the flesh; this was the mark of Cain that exposed those who had sought cover in the stolen uniforms of less guilty branches of the German forces. One man, exposed in this way, yelled out in protest, turning to the men behind him for support, but was greeted with indifference, even flickers of *Schadenfreude*.

An orderly sprayed them for lice, the fine white powder a cloud of humiliation that hung about them for a few seconds before settling on skin and clothing. Ubi breathed it in, and coughed and spat to rid himself of the chemical taste. He felt like an animal, prodded, probed, and treated for infestation before re-joining the herd of milling figures, clustering together like cattle.

And everywhere he saw the raw hopelessness of defeat, only punctuated now and then by thoughts of how much worse it would have been had it been the Russians who had overrun them. The Russians were bent on revenge, shooting their captives out of hand or waiting for starvation, or death by thirst, to do their work for them; one of the men who had been on the eastern front told them of a unit of Georgian cannibals that had been let loose on German prisoners. They chose the youngest men, the boys of fifteen, even younger, who had been drafted in as the ranks of their elders were steadily diminished. "This happened," he said. "I saw it. They ate the boys."

Ubi did not believe him. Men went mad in war, he thought, but not that mad. Such stories had been put about by the authorities to persuade people to fight when they had lost all enthusiasm for the cause. Ubi had never wanted to fight in the first place. His elder brother had been a communist and had told him that this war was nothing to do with the people of Germany but was fratricidal lunacy inspired by a demented

Austrian. His brother had expressed these views once too often, and in the wrong company, and disappeared without trace one morning. That left Ubi with a mother and a sister, his father having died a few months after the war began.

His mother and his sister were in Berlin, and when news filtered through that the city had fallen to the Russians he sat with his head in his hands, trying as hard as he could not to think about what would happen to them. It was unbearable, and he eventually told himself that they had both been killed, in their sleep, by a direct hit by an American bomb on their flat in Wedding. An American bomb would have been clean and merciful, and they would not have suffered – unlike those who found themselves in the path of Ivan.

They were marched from one place to another, and eventually he found himself being called out at early morning muster and taken to a tent in which a Canadian major, flanked by an interpreter, quizzed him about his service record. There was not much to say, of course; he had had a quiet war, and had not so much as fired a shot in anger. He did not bother to tell his interrogator this, as it sounded such an unlikely story, and anyway would already have been used by those with most to hide.

But that was not what the Canadian wanted to find out.

"We've had information," the major said, referring to a typewritten sheet before him, "that you were of assistance to two American airmen. Can you tell me a bit more about that?"

He hesitated. He did not want to stand out from the crowd in any way. He wanted to be anonymous, just to be one of the hundreds of thousands of defeated soldiers who could not be individually punished for what had happened. He wanted

to go home. He wanted to take off this uniform and escape
from under the rank cloud that the army carried with it: in
good times a miasma of cruelty and noise and raucous singing,
and now, in defeat, a dark air of gloom and brokenness. He
wanted to sit with a girl in a café and drink coffee and feel the
sunlight; he wanted to lie in a bath of soapy water; he wanted
to clean and bind the recalcitrant ulcer that had developed on
his right foot; he wanted not to smell. Would that ever again be
possible? The world was in ruins; there would be no medicines
for the dregs of this disgraced army; coffee would be a distant
memory; and what would girls want to do with the men whom
they would blame for bringing this all about?

"Well, tell me," prompted the major. "What assistance did
you provide?"

He saw that the major had cut himself while shaving and
had applied a styptic pencil to the nick.

"I took food," he said.

The major stared at him. "You didn't report them?"

He shook his head. He was tired. What was the point of
going over the things that had happened in war? The dead
stayed dead; the living preferred to forget. Did anything else
really matter?

"So, you didn't report them and you took them food? Why
did you do this?"

He shrugged. "The war was almost over," he said. "And I
didn't see any point."

He felt the major's eyes on him. He looked away. He wanted
this interview to come to an end.

The major turned to the interpreter and said to him, in
English, "Is this man telling the truth?"

The interpreter answered, "Yes, I think so. I can't be sure, sir, but liars talk in a different way – it's just something they do. This man isn't doing that."

The major laughed. "I wish I had your certainty. Mind-reader, are you?"

"It's all there on that piece of paper," pointed out the interpreter. "He seems to be confirming it."

The major turned back to Ubi. "We are sending home a number of prisoners," he said. "They are either very sick or very deserving – mostly sick, although heaven knows what they can do for them back in Germany. A smaller number are men who have done something to help us – men like you. There are very few of those, I might add."

Ubi listened.

"You live in Berlin?"

"Yes."

"Would you like to go back there? The Soviets . . ."

"But you are there too, I hear."

The major nodded. "The Americans, yes. The British and the French too. You can go if you wish."

He collected his few possessions – a kit bag, a spare shirt that he had tried to launder in cold water.

"Don't tell the other men you're leaving," the major had warned him. "Say that you're being transferred to another prisoner-of-war camp. They might not take it too well."

When he went back to the major's tent, he was told to take off his clothes and change into a new set of clothing they provided for him. The trousers were too large, but he was given an old tie to serve as belt. They were at least clean, as was the shirt they gave him. There were even fresh underclothes, fastened with drawstrings because elastic was hard to come by. His old clothing was picked up by a Canadian corporal, his face distorted with unconcealed distaste, and thrown on the ground outside.

"Burn all that," snapped the major. "Don't leave it there, for God's sake."

The corporal went outside and gestured to a soldier to fetch a can of petrol. A few drops were sprinkled on the clothing and a match applied. Ubi was surprised at the size of the flames that enveloped his abandoned clothing, and the smoke too. It was his past that was in flames, he thought, and he was grateful. He was cleansed. He had fresh clothing and was being taken back to Germany, taken home, to find out whether his mother and sister were still alive.

"You're a fortunate man," said the major.

Ubi knew he was right. He wanted to thank the officer for what he had done, but he could not get the words out. Words, it seemed, had deserted him, as if his brain sensed that there was no point in trying to express the immensity of what had happened. Only two reactions to war seemed possible: a silence, as of horror, or a wail of anguish.

"You're fortunate because you're no longer in uniform," the major went on. "These men . . ." He gestured to the corporal and a guard standing at the entrance to the tent. "These men are still in uniform."

Now Ubi found his voice. "You are very kind, sir."

The major sighed. "Doing my job, that's all." He gave Ubi a piece of paper impressed with an official stamp. "You are no longer a prisoner of war," he said. "You are demobilised, as of now. You are a civilian again."

They took him away with two other men. One had a bandaged head and looked dazed and unsure what was happening. The other seemed to be uninjured, but muttered incessantly under his breath in a heavy, unfamiliar dialect. They were driven to another army post, where they waited several hours before being loaded, with other men, into an army truck just as night was descending. The back of the truck was closed, and they saw nothing. One of the men started to sing one of the songs they had been taught, the *Westerwaldlied*, but this was greeted with scowls, and he stopped halfway through a line, awkward and embarrassed.

They were transferred onto a train late at night, into an open wagon into which a few blankets had been tossed. They were not told where the train was going, other than Germany; they would have to make their way home from wherever it was that it stopped. After what seemed like an interminable wait, the engine started its journey; he tried to settle, lying down on one of the blankets, but the train jolted and squeaked and sleep eluded him. Lying awake, he looked sideways through a gap in the slats that made up the side of the wagon, watching such lights as the battered towns possessed. There was an acrid smell; the train had been used for transporting lignite, and his new clothes were soon discoloured with the dust of the cheap coal. He did not care. He was returning to Germany, and whatever had happened to it, it was still Germany; it was still his country.

19

With his release document in his hand, Ubi considered himself lucky: others lingered far longer than he as prisoners or forced labourers, and many succumbed, particularly those who fell into the hands of the Russians. Yet he had a feeling of being cast adrift, at the beginning of a journey that would be long, complicated, and beset with bureaucratic obstacles. The original release paper, so potent in getting him on that train back to Germany, would have a great deal of work to do, and he feared it would soon lose its power. There were just too many displaced persons; there were just too many ration books and travel passes to be issued for much time to be spent on the claims of one young man who had been released early and simply wanted to get back to a home that probably no longer existed. A whole country had been uprooted and turned upside down; everybody was looking for somebody, and the ether was full of echoing, plaintive cries: *ich suche meine Frau; ich suche meinen Sohn* – I am looking for my wife; I am looking for my son. Scraps of paper were pinned on notice boards, half obscuring one another like the over-abundant leaves of trees in full foliage, each a record of a desperate attempt to find out what had happened to sons, to brothers, to husbands. *Do you know anybody who was at Stalingrad? Did anybody ever mention a Sergeant Kurt Muller from Hamburg, who was posted there?*

Prisoners of war were fed, but those, like Ubi, who were demobilised had to find work if they were to eat. He had no idea whether his mother and sister were still alive; he had not heard from them and he had found out that the street on which they lived in Berlin had been reduced to rubble. Stories of the atrocities suffered at the hands of the Russians had filtered through: whispered accounts of rape on an unremittingly brutal scale. They said that the bodies of those who were killed had simply disappeared under the broken buildings and would never be recovered. The rats grew fat on this hidden bounty – their tunnels reached places where the efforts of those clearing the ruins would never penetrate. People said that it was a place of silence, like a city of the dead, shocked by the fate it had brought upon itself.

That first train journey had ended on a station in a small city that had got off fairly lightly in the bombing raids. Almost three-quarters of it was intact, and there was food too, as it was a market town for the surrounding countryside. Although there was no coal, the woods nearby provided wood for fuel, and people brought this into town each afternoon on hand carts loaded with bark and hand-sawn timber.

The population was less dispersed than in places where the physical destruction had been worse. Yet even so, there were few men, and certainly not enough men of Ubi's age to do the work that needed to be done. He had been intending to join the streams of people he had seen heading to a nearby larger city, but on his first morning he was approached by a woman at the railway station. She asked him whether he could help her: she owned an inn, she said; her husband had been on the eastern front and there was no word of him. "I don't think he will be back," she said. "I like to tell myself otherwise, but I am a realist."

He lowered his eyes. Was she blaming him, in some way, for what had happened? Her tone had been almost accusing, and he thought she might imagine him to be a party member, or an SS man, or something that he had not been.

"In what way do you think I can help?" he asked.

"I need somebody to help me at the inn," she said. "I need somebody to do the man's work. To fix things."

She mentioned that the person who helped her would get a warm room – it was above the kitchen – and his keep. "I have food," she said. "My inn is being used by British officers who are billeted there. Not fighting people – administrators. They're the new government, you see. I prepare their rations." She looked at him meaningfully. "I prepare their rations," she repeated.

Hunger gnawed at his stomach. He had not eaten for eighteen hours, and from somewhere in the station there came the smell of soup. He was dirty.

"I even have hot water," said the woman. "Not much, but enough."

He met her gaze. "I want to get back to Berlin," he said.

She looked at him as if he had said something beyond comprehension. "Berlin is full of Russians," she said. "And it's surrounded."

"I'd like to go eventually."

"But not now?"

"Maybe not now."

She smiled. "So you'll work for me?"

He nodded. He was tired.

They walked back to the inn, which was not far from the station. A British military car was parked outside it, a Union Jack pennant limp in the lifeless air.

"That's the English colonel's car," said the woman. "He has

an office next to his room. He prefers to work there."

He nodded. "Do they pay you?"

"Not what I would like, but something. It means I can keep the inn open – most of the others have closed."

She showed him to his room. Her name, she told him, was Ilse Marten. Her father had been a Lutheran pastor, she said, and he had died four years before the war began. "I am glad he died then," she said. "He was spared the worst of the monster who got us into this."

"This war?"

She looked at him cautiously; she had spoken freely, but now ancient habit reasserted itself. There were still fanatics who had not changed their views and one had to be circumspect in what one said. He put her mind at rest. "It's a pity they didn't hang him," he muttered. "They got the others – or a lot of them – but he cheated them."

She looked relieved. "Well, that settles that," she said. "If you make a fire under the boiler you can have some hot water. I have a razor you can use, if you like – it was my husband's."

He mumbled something. What was there to say, beyond the trite expressions of sympathy?

As she had promised, his room was warm, the heat coming from the flue of the kitchen range directly below. This was exposed as it passed up through his room, and there was warmth, too, that came up through the floorboards, along with cooking smells. He later learned that there was coal – it was not meant for civilians, but the British officers were entitled to it and they passed it on to Ilse for kitchen use.

He took off his socks and felt the warmth underfoot. It took him back to Holland, where they had enjoyed an ample supply of wood for heating their barracks. Defeat had been cold; it had been hunger and cold.

"You may have a bath," said Ilse. "I have run the water for you. And there is soap."

He had not seen soap for weeks and he handled it now as if it were something precious. In the bath he noticed that he was changing colour as the grime came off; it was as if he were shedding a skin.

She entered the room with a towel, unconcerned at his nakedness. Nobody seemed to worry about such things any longer; modesty was unimportant when survival was at stake.

The towel was clean and smelled of something he could not quite place. And then he remembered: it was lavender. It was one of the familiar smells that had simply gone from his memory, replaced by the overpowering smells of war: smoke, burning rubber, the stink of putrefaction. There was even a smell for fear – a sharp, uneasy tang that was something to do with the sweat of frightened men. And now the smell of lavender came back to him, and as he pressed the towel to his face he felt the urge to weep. There was so much to bring tears: the loss of those years of his youth when he should have been happy; his recruitment into a cause of rampage and killing; the pain of others; the humiliation of defeat. He was nothing: the conquerors were here, among them, and he and so many like him counted for nothing.

He went downstairs, where she gave him a bowl of soup. He sat at the kitchen table and tried to control his hunger; it would not do to sink this in a single draught, which is what he wanted to do. He did not want her to think he was that desperate. But he was, and the soup took seconds to disappear.

She was watching, half amused, half pitying. "Let your stomach get used to food," she said. "They say that you can do damage if you eat too much too quickly."

He nodded. "I have been so hungry."

She smiled at him, and poured a small second helping of soup into the bowl. "They expect us to survive on less than half of what they get," she said. "I've seen it in print – in black and white. Our ration is meant to be one thousand calories a day. We don't get even that."

He stared into the soup bowl. Now it was all charity – every scrap came at the will of those put in authority over them. And yet, he thought, this is our payback. This is what we started, if it was indeed true that we started it. He could not remember. There were vague claims; had Poland provoked Germany? Had it been necessary to attack the Russians because of what they were doing to Germans who had the misfortune to live in the east?

She was saying something to him about work, and he stopped thinking of issues of retribution. He apologised. "I'm sorry – I wasn't listening."

She explained that if he felt strong enough, there was wood to be chopped. She had bought a load of felled oak from a man she knew but the pieces were too large to fit into the stove. And then there was a window that needed repairing. She had managed to get her hands on a piece of glass that should fit – it was probably stolen from somebody else, but if you started asking questions nowadays you would never get anything done. Everything was stolen, and had he heard: the Russians had removed everything, even things that were bolted down, and sent it back to Russia – whole factories, cranes, even small buildings that could be dismantled and shipped off. And people too, of course; they were easy to transport: you simply loaded them into the wagons of a train and then unloaded those who were still alive at the other end. Siberia, or somewhere.

"Mind you . . ." she said.

He waited. Mind you, what?

"Mind you, the colonel has shown me photographs that you wouldn't believe. Our people doing the same thing. Packing people off to camps in the east. They died there, you know." She paused. "He had photographs. They're making people – civilians – look at the photographs. Then they say: *See this? See what you people did?*"

He looked away. He would never have allowed anything like that. If there was a stain, then it was not on his hands.

He started work after the meal. At four o'clock that afternoon, some of the officers who were billeted on the hotel returned from work. One of them looked at him with distaste, and threw an enquiring look at Ilse. She shook her head.

"He was never in the army or anything," she said in English. She searched for the English word – was there one? "Asthma." She pointed at Ubi's chest.

He did not understand, but the officer merely raised an eyebrow and went off to his room.

Ilse turned to Ubi and told him what she had said. "It's simpler that they don't know," she said. "Especially that one. He likes young men and it's best for you if he thinks you're . . ." She tapped her chest. "Understand?"

He tried to work out Ilse's age. Ubi was just twenty-three, and he thought that she must be somewhere in her thirties. But two days after he arrived she told him that she was coming up to her twenty-eighth birthday. She had married when she was twenty, and had experienced barely five years of marriage before her husband had been conscripted into the army. She had managed to run the inn by herself, with the help of the staff who had been there since before they bought it; but then those people had retired, or moved for various reasons connected with the war, and she had been obliged to work longer and longer hours. At length it had been only her and two part-time chambermaids, which was why Ubi's arrival was so welcome.

It did not take him long to settle in. The regular meals, the security of being host to the occupying forces, and the warmth and comfort of his room made him happy to stay where he was and not think about going on to Berlin. Winter was approaching, and people said that it would be severe. They said that rations would be reduced and that the slow march of starvation would devour whole swathes of Germany. It was no time to be doing anything adventurous; far better to put up with the tedium of the wood-cutting and the other mundane tasks he was expected to perform. It would be madness to go to Berlin at this point, Ilse said; the Russians could seize him on any grounds, or no grounds at all, and spirit him off to a factory or a mine in the Soviet Union. That had happened to hundreds of thousands of Germans, they said; men who were now working in Soviet coal mines or on building sites, repairing the wrecked towns and cities. They would need more as these men, undernourished and badly housed, died in droves. If you go to Berlin, she said, then that will be you.

He realised that there would be work to do on the inn itself. Little maintenance had been done for years, the neglect going back to a time well before the war. There was a barn at the back, full of old agricultural implements, and behind it, half covered by a frayed tarpaulin, some sort of round wooden structure that intrigued him. It was like a vast towering vat, a straight-sided wine barrel, perhaps, the height of at least three men, and of vast capacity. There was lettering on the side of it, but it was difficult, with the tarpaulin and the effect of weathering, to make out what this said.

On the second day he asked her. "That thing out there. That big barrel."

They were standing in the kitchen, where he was drying plates before stacking them on the shelves.

She smiled. "Big barrel? I suppose you could call it that."

He waited for the explanation. She had moved over to the window and was looking out towards the barn.

"It's a *Motodrom*," she said. "It's a fairground thing. You ride your motorcycle round and round and then you go up the wall and you carry on going round and round on that. You defy gravity. Fairground stuff."

The shape, the writing: of course.

"I know what a *Motodrom* is," he said. "I've seen one before."

"Well, that's what that is."

He shook his head in disbelief. "You have a *Motodrom* . . ."

"It's pretty decrepit. It hasn't been used for years."

He looked out of the window towards the barn. "Amazing. A *Motodrom*. You know, when I was a boy there were fairground people who came to Berlin. They must have been from somewhere deep in the south, because they spoke with a very broad Bavarian accent. You'd think they were singing half the time. They had a *Motodrom*. I used to spend my pocket money on tickets to watch them. I loved it."

She looked at him indulgently. "I suppose that when you're a boy, something like that is very exciting."

"It was. It was the most exciting thing I'd ever seen."

"I can imagine that," she said. "Noise. Danger. Speed. The things that boys like." And men, she thought; hence this war.

"I thought then," Ubi continued, "when I was a boy, that is, that I'd give anything – anything – to have a *Motodrom*. I thought it would be the finest thing in the world to own a *Motodrom*."

Ilse laughed. "I'll sell you mine. Not that you – or anybody else – would want to buy it." Then she said, "You know what the English officers call it? It's called a wall of death over there, they told me. One of them was interested in it. The fat one with the moustache. He said he'd seen one in England and that's what they called it."

Ubi asked where it came from.

"It belonged to my husband's uncle. He had no children and he left it to him. My husband said he'd get it going again one day. The uncle always said there was good money in it."

"He'd ride it himself?"

She came back from the window and looked at him in a way that conveyed that she did not wish to talk about her husband.

The knowledge that he had somewhere to stay – and the sense of security this brought – meant that the fractured, fitful sleep patterns that had been with him since his conscription were fading, and his nights becoming restful once again. He began to look forward to the moment when he finished the washing up after the evening meal – a task that Ilse had been eager to off-load – and he could go up to his room, throw off his clothes, and sink into the haven of laundered sheets and a down mattress. It was unfathomable luxury for him after army beds, and then no bed at all. The dreams that came to him were vague and confused: he was in Holland, then he was somewhere else altogether, in a landscape he did not recognise; he was back at school, writing in an exercise book, dimly aware that he was being tested in some way; he was in the company of his brother who had gone missing, who in his dream embraced him and told him that everything was all right, even though he was dead.

In a vivid dream that recurred from time to time he was in the presence of someone powerful. They were walking somewhere and the other person was singing some little song under his breath, chopping at wildflowers with a walking stick. And he knew his name – that was the astonishing thing; he called him Ubi and asked him if he had anything he wanted to say to him. Was this the Führer himself? Surely not, because he knew Ubi's name and he looked different, although he was wearing something that looked like a uniform.

He told Ilse about these dreams one day and she said that it was very common to dream about their vanished leaders. "So many people have told me this happens to them," she said. "It's because they penetrated our lives so deeply. You dream of things like that, you know."

"And you?" he asked. "Do you dream about them too?"

She shook her head. "Not that I know of. But then they say, don't they, that everyone has his particular nightmares."

"And yours?" he asked.

She hesitated before answering. "The Jews," she said. "I dream about the Jews."

He watched her. He saw her lower her eyes.

"We murdered them," she said. "We took their houses, their businesses, everything. Then we sent them away to be killed."

He did not say anything. People were only just beginning to talk about these things, and many simply refused to believe them. How could so many people be disposed of in that way? Surely it was impossible.

But he knew it was true. "It happened," he said.

She met his eyes. "It's our fault," she said. "We all became murderers. And it was not just the Jews – it was the Gypsies and the insane and all sorts of people. All marched off to be killed."

He wanted to do something for her evident pain. "You didn't do it personally," he said. "You're only accountable for things you do personally."

She wanted to believe him, but it seemed to her that the crime was just too big; it required a whole nation to commit something on that scale. "There were some Jews here, you know," she said. "The party people painted signs on their doors. They broke their windows. I saw some of them doing it; I saw them from my kitchen window. And what did I do? Nothing. I stood and watched."

"You would have got into trouble if you'd tried to do anything," Ubi said. "People were sent to prison for less."

"Oh, I know that," she said, suddenly sounding weary. "But the fact remains that I did nothing. And now we're paying for that. All this hardship is because of what we started."

"We can begin again," said Ubi. "They might make us pay, but they can't make us all pay with our lives."

She was staring at him. "You're ready to start again?" she asked.

"Of course. And Germany will start up again. You watch."

"I'm watching," she said wearily.

There were ten officers billeted at the inn. Five of them spoke German – two of them with a facility approaching the fluency of a native speaker. One was an intelligence officer; the others were part of the military government for that part of the British sector. They were mostly concerned with mundane matters – transport and provisions, criminal justice; two had been lawyers in civilian life and now found themselves dealing with the crimes of desperate people – and with the control of disease. Theft had become an almost natural response to shortage; if you were hungry, you stole – there was a simple, inarguable logic to that response. People who were not prepared to steal died. But they perished, too, of typhus and dysentery, and of sheer neglect; they died because nobody cared very much for them, not even their fellow citizens.

One of the German-speaking officers asked Ubi whether he would like to learn English. "I could teach you," he said. "I'm sure you'll be a quick learner. And, as payment, you can help me with my German – I still get things wrong from time to time. And people are always using colloquial expressions that I've never come across before. It would be helpful to learn a few more of those."

He readily agreed, and the lessons were conducted each day in the twenty minutes before dinner. Ilse liked to work in the kitchen by herself, and did not ask Ubi to help. "You'll have plenty to do once the plates are cleared," she said.

He sat with the officer in the small parlour at the front of the inn. The officer had a book that he lent to Ubi; it had pictures of everyday things in it with the English nouns printed below.

"A hat," said Ubi, pointing to a picture of a man in a bowler hat, under which the word *hat* appeared.

The man was looking towards the camera and smiling broadly. Ubi switched to German: "He doesn't look guilty, does he?"

The officer looked surprised. "Why should he look guilty?" he asked.

Ubi shrugged. "I suppose it's because so many people look guilty. I suppose I've come to expect it." He paused. "But then the man in this picture is English, isn't he?"

"I think so," said the officer. "Look at the red buses in the background. That's always a giveaway, I find."

"The English have nothing to feel guilty about," said Ubi.

The officer smiled. "Nice of you to say that," he said. "But we also have a history, you know."

Ubi stared at the officer. His face was unremarkable, although there was a certain pleasing regularity to it. His eyes were clear, and he looked straight at you when he spoke. That was an ability that came with never having done anything he was ashamed of, thought Ubi.

There was a picture of a family drinking tea. Each person, and each item, was labelled with the appropriate English word: *father, mother, son, daughter; cup, saucer, teaspoon*; and so on. Through the window could be seen a *tree* and a *hill*. It was a world that seemed to suit the softer nature of the words, even if *Vater* and *Mutter* clearly came from the same place as *father* and *mother*. This was not a language to shout in, thought Ubi; this was not a language with which to articulate threats, or invade, or terrify others.

He was a quick learner, and he was soon able to read the

cyclostyled newsletters that the British prepared for their own troops. The officer helped him with this, encouraging and complimenting as he stumbled through the easily smudged text. There was piece about fraternization; a warning not to trust German civilians.

"Do not talk to these people," read Ubi, enunciating each word carefully. These people . . . Who were these people? *Me?*

The officer looked apologetic and switched to German to explain. "They don't really mean ordinary people. They mean people who might have been SS or something like that. People who haven't accepted the outcome. That's what this means."

"But it says ordinary civilians," said Ubi.

"We don't follow rules in quite the same way as you people do," said the officer. And then, as if to himself, "That's the trouble. I mean, the trouble with you people, so to speak."

And then, looking out of the window, and as if talking to himself rather than to Ubi, the officer continued, "I don't want to be here, you know. Like most people, I don't want to be here at all."

"But if you weren't here," said Ubi, "wouldn't it be even more terrible?"

The next two years passed quickly for Ubi. He was kept busy in the inn, and soon became indispensable not only in the kitchen, but in the performance of a range of maintenance tasks. He became skilled in woodwork and in plumbing, and even managed to fathom and sort out the building's antiquated electrical wiring. He generally kept to himself; the war had been a waking nightmare and now he wanted nothing so much as the peace and quiet of a modest, uncomplicated life. In April

1948 he had news of his family, thanks to the help of the officer who had been teaching him English. He used contacts in the British sector in Berlin to make enquiries on Ubi's behalf, and came up with the address of the landlord who had owned the building in which they had lived. This man responded, and told him that unfortunately his mother had been killed when a mortar shell came through the window in May 1945. His sister had gone to live with one of the other residents – a widow – and had stayed there until quite recently. He was sorry to report that she had become ill – it was typhus, he believed – and she, too, had died. She had a young child, he said, and the widow had looked after the little boy. The widow had moved, but he had her address as she had done some work for him and he was still in touch with her. She had a small job and she was hard up, but the boy was still with her, he thought.

Ilse found him in the kitchen with the letter on the table in front of him. There was a pile of onion skins beside it, and when she saw his tears she smiled. "Don't you know what to do?" she chided. "When you're peeling onions, you should have a tap running nearby. It stops you crying."

She laughed, and scooped the onions skins away to put in the compost. And then she realised her mistake.

He gestured to the letter, inviting her to pick it up. She read the first few sentences and then dropped it back on the table. She put her arms around him. "Ubi, Ubi . . ." Somehow, in that moment, she felt that the sorrows of Germany had crystallised, and she wept too – not just for this woman and her daughter, who were just two amongst millions, but for everything, for all the hatred and injustice and revenge; for all the immeasurable pain.

He told her that he should get back to Berlin, even if only to see what remained of their home, which might be nothing but an empty space; in pictures, Berlin looked a wasteland, a place in which troglodytes eked out an existence in the basements of ruins. Ilse tried to dissuade him, but she knew that he had to go. She had heard that from so many others, who had said that they were drawn back to the place where it happened, to the site of their loss.

"And there's a child," he added. "My sister's child. I must see him." He was virtually alone now; he had lost all his family and this unknown child was all he had.

"Of course you must."

"I feel responsible, you see."

A few weeks earlier he and Ilse had become lovers, shyly and with very little being said about it. He had worked for her for over two years, and had become indispensable about the inn. He had repaired the roof – a task that took over eight months – and had replaced rotten timbers on the ground floor, scouring bombsites for wood, shaping each by hand. It was comfort and tenderness that lay at the heart of their relationship, rather than passion. It was as if they were children lost in a wood, holding onto one another in the darkness.

"If you go to Berlin," she said, "will you come back here?"

She did not say "come back to me", as she did not want him to feel trapped.

He replied that he would. "Of course I shall." And then he said, "And I'll ask you to marry me then."

She hardly dared speak, but she managed to say, "Can I?"

"Because of . . ." She hardly ever mentioned her husband, but he knew that he was called Erik. "Because of Erik?"

She nodded. "I suppose he's dead, but . . ."

"I think he must be."

It was as if his words were an official confirmation. "Then in that case, I can," she said.

They left the discussion at that. He told her that he would be no more than a few weeks in Berlin and would be back before she knew it. She smiled, and kissed his forehead gently. She said a prayer, silently, because she believed in God and she thought that he did not.

"You can bring the child back," she whispered. "There's room for a child here."

He stared at her, moved by her generosity. That had been evident from the very first day, when she had accosted him at the station, and it had continued: the soups, the comfortable bed, the laundering of his shirts, the bottles of Burgundy diverted from the supplies of the British officers. "Are you sure?"

"Of course."

"I don't know anything about him," said Ubi. "I don't even know who the father is." An unspoken word hung in the air between them: *Russian*.

On the evening before he was due to leave, one of the British officers, a newly arrived one – they were always changing – removed the tarpaulin from the abandoned *Motodrom*. Several of his fellow officers joined him, some still in uniform, having just come off duty. They shouted to one another, and their laughter drifted back to the inn, where Ubi and Ilse were watching from a window.

Ubi turned to Ilse. "Did they ask you?"

She shrugged. "One said something about taking a look at it. Not that young one. The one with the bad skin – he asked me."

Ubi wondered what they intended to do, and was about to ask her when he heard the motorcycle. One of the younger officers appeared from round the side of the building, riding an army motorbike.

He looked at Ilse. "Do you think . . ."

"They'd be mad," she said. "But then the British are mad – everybody knows that."

The officers had managed to open a door in the side of the *Motodrom*. The motorbike was now driven up to this and the rider dismounted and pushed it inside.

Ilse opened the window at which she and Ubi were standing. She shouted out towards the officers. "Careful. That's very dangerous."

The officers waved back gaily, but paid no attention.

They heard the sound of the motorbike engine reverberating inside the *Motodrom*, and then a thud, followed by silence.

Laughter broke the silence, followed by raucous shouting, and then more laughter.

"Boys," said Ilse. And then she thought about the war, and she thought *boys* again.

20

He had been prepared for the destruction he found in Berlin, although people he met there kept telling him how bad it had been a few years back, in 1945. "You wouldn't believe it," said the only one of his friends from school he managed to locate. Stoffi suffered from asthma and that had saved his life, as he had been given a wireless operator's job that kept him far from the front line, almost up to the end. "You wouldn't believe the stench, Ubi. Everywhere. Weeks, months of stench, because many of the Russians, the real peasants, came from places where there was no proper sanitation and they didn't know. The other thing they didn't know about was watches. They'd never had watches and so they stole every watch they could get their hands on. They wore them all the way up their arms – five or six under each sleeve. But you couldn't laugh at them when they rolled their sleeves up and the watches appeared, because they could fly into a rage without any warning. Anywhere. Everywhere. You wouldn't believe it, Ubi; you wouldn't."

At first, he listened without making any comment of his own. Invasion – defeat – was a brute fact about which one could say very little, even if one was the guiltless victim. But in our case, he thought, we are far from guiltless and so can say even less. We did it to them, and now they're doing it to us. Who could blame the Russians?

"We're surrounded," said Stoffi. "And they'll turn the screws. Of course they will."

"But what can they do? What about the others? The Americans? The British? The French?"

Stoffi shrugged. "They're surrounded too – at least in Berlin. They say the Russians are already making it more difficult for them to reach us here. They say that bridges are being repaired, or railway lines need work – that sort of thing." He paused, to make a strangling motion with his hands. "They could squeeze us just like that, you know."

At least the streets were now clear of rubble. The burnt cars had been removed and rebuilding had long since started. There were people on the streets and they seemed to have proper shoes – or many of them did – and the trams and trains were running. The furtiveness that he had noticed in the early days of defeat seemed less common here; people walked, rather than scurried; they looked one another in the eye, rather than shiftily, warily; there were political notices and newspapers. There were still echoes of hopelessness – that indefinable air with which he had become so familiar – but there was something else now, something quite different: a sense of a future. People were doing things purposively; they were doing things that seemed to matter to them; Germany was making things again and these things were beginning to appear in shops.

Stoffi allowed him to sleep on the floor of the basement room he occupied. He gave him food and accompanied him when he went to look for the widow whose address he had been given.

"People move a lot these days," Stoffi warned Ubi. "Don't be too disappointed if you find this woman has gone."

But she had not. She answered the door in a neat apron, her hands covered with flour. She had been kneading dough.

He told her who he was, and for a few moments she stared

at him in confusion. Then, as she made sense of what he had said, she raised her hands to her face. When she lowered them, there were traces of flour on her eyebrows and cheekbones. She sat down heavily on a chair in the entrance hall and shook her head.

"I thought you were all gone," she said. "All of you."

He told her that he had been taken prisoner and had been released early. He told her how he had obtained her address.

"I thought I should see my nephew," he explained. "I think my sister would have wanted that."

"Of course, of course. Your nephew . . ."

He waited. Children had died too, many of them from malnutrition. Was he too late?

She stood up. "Your nephew will be coming back very soon. A friend of mine has taken him to the shops. He won't be long."

She invited them in. The flat was neat, but spartan in its furnishing and decoration. Poverty manifested itself in the absence of anything of any value; people had sold their possessions in difficult times. A family heirloom might have been exchanged for a few loaves of bread; an item of jewellery – a ring, a brooch – could have brought in a few kilos of donkey meat.

As he waited, he tried to make conversation. He asked about what had happened to his mother and his sister, but she was able to tell him very little. She had been somewhere else when his mother's flat had been hit; and his sister, whom she did not know very well, had died rather quickly. She had taken the child in because there did not seem to be anybody else and it was her duty, she said, as a Christian. She did not know where either of them was buried; so many people, she said, had shallow graves that were either unmarked or only temporarily recorded. He asked the widow about the days after the Russians had arrived, but she clearly did not want to talk about that. She shuddered, though, involuntarily, and then started to discuss a Russian film she had seen the previous day. It had been beautifully filmed, she said, and if it had been propaganda, then that side of it had been lost on her, as she had no Russian.

The friend returned with the boy half an hour later. She was carrying a large paper bag into which groceries had been stuffed; at her feet, clinging onto her skirts, was a small boy of about three. He was wearing a tight-fitting cap that failed to cover his ears and a shabby red coat, and he stared at Ubi and Stoffi with the unembarrassed curiosity of the very young.

The child was dark-skinned, his black hair knotted with small curls.

Ubi smiled at the boy, and then looked at the widow. She held his gaze, almost defiantly, as if she were daring him to say something.

"What's his name?" he asked.

"Klaus," she said.

Ubi stepped forward and bent down to address the child at his level. He reached out for the boy's right hand, and held it briefly in his own. "So you're Klaus," he said. "And I'm your uncle."

The boy looked at the widow, as if to ask permission to respond. She smiled encouragingly, but he was too timid to say anything.

Ubi stood up again. The widow stepped back; she had been about to whisper something into his ear. "An American father," she said.

He looked at the child again. "I see."

She nodded. "It was not easy for your sister," she said. "People abused her because of the child's being mixed race. Some people actually spat at her."

His chest felt tight. "This man . . . the father . . . was she . . ."

The widow knew what he was trying to ask. "No, don't think that. She said he was kind to her. And people had to make whatever arrangements they could in those times, you know."

He let out his breath slowly. "Did he know about the child?"

The widow shrugged. "He may have – I don't know. Your sister told me that he had been sent somewhere else. He was a sergeant. She showed me a photograph."

The child was watching him with widened eyes. He reached into his pocket and took out a small bar of chocolate, which he unwrapped. He offered it to the small boy, who hesitated, and then took it from him.

"We need to talk," said Ubi.

The widow nodded. "I would appreciate it if you were able to help in some way."

"I'll take him," said Ubi. "If you don't mind letting him go, I'll take him back with me. I have a place to live, and I'm going to be getting married. We shall look after him well."

The widow hesitated, but not for long. "I would have been happy to continue," she said. "I would never have turned him out, but it's such a struggle to get by . . ." She looked at him hopelessly. It was a miracle, it seemed to him, that people managed to continue. From somewhere within themselves they found the will to persist, to scrape a living, to patch and mend, to find small ways of expressing their sense of beauty – a few flowers plucked and put in a cracked egg cup serving as a vase; a printed picture cut from a magazine and pasted on cardboard; a splash of colour in a threadbare dress.

He reached out and touched her arm. "I understand," he said. "And I'm very grateful to you – I really am."

"You have work back there?" she asked. "Real work?" The labour draft had sucked up able-bodied men for construction, but the pay was minimal.

He told her about the inn. "My fiancée" – it was the first time he had used the word of Ilse – "my fiancée owns it."

"Ah."

He noticed a change in her expression. Was it envy? When most had nothing, the possession of something had to be concealed. So he said, "It's not a big place. It's a very modest concern. Just a few rooms."

He was right; it had been envy, because the look disappeared.

"Klaus will be well fed," he said.

She prickled with resentment. "I've done my best on what I get."

He was quick to reassure her. "I'm sure you have. And he looks very healthy, doesn't he?"

He did not, and they both knew it. But she accepted the compliment, and then turned to Stoffi and asked him where he lived. Ubi bent down again to speak to the child, who continued to look at him with his wide, dark eyes, wondering whether to trust him. The chocolate had gone, leaving a smudge on the boy's upper lip. Ubi reached into his pocket and took out another bar, handing it over with a flourish. This brought a shy grin to the small face as his nephew reached out to take possession of the treasure.

They agreed that Ubi would leave the following week, once the child had had the chance to get used to his company. He would visit each day, and familiarity – and chocolate – would do its work. But as the day of departure approached, so its possibility receded. The boy had no papers, and the widow, at whose address he was registered for ration purposes, lived in the Soviet zone. Just as Stoffi had said, road and rail transport between Berlin and the outside world was now being deliberately cut by the Russians, as were transfers of food from the countryside to the non-Soviet zones of the city.

"Stalin has two big weapons," said Stoffi. "Starvation and isolation. Watch him use them. Just watch him. There is nothing that man would not do."

They attended a meeting – an impromptu gathering of neighbours addressed by a local liaison official. Somebody, a thin man wearing horn-rimmed glasses, brandished a French newspaper, with its headline *Berlin crisis: a challenge for the West.* "They say here that America's going to give up," he said. "That's what the French think. Listen."

He read out a few sentences, which he translated into German.

"The French!" called a woman from the back of the crowd. "What do they know? They're defeated, just like us."

"Not quite," said the liaison man. "But the Americans are not going to abandon us. There's an agreement."

This brought laughter.

"No," shouted the official. "No, you're wrong. General Clay isn't going to let it happen."

"What can he do?" someone shouted.

"They can force their way in."

"With tanks?" That'll be a war between America and Russia. And we'll be in the middle."

A voice at the front said, "The way we were not all that long ago."

Other views were expressed. "General Clay won't risk that. He knows what the Russians are like." And "There's not much he can do. Look at the number of Russian tanks – they say they're bringing more in every day. Piling them up. America's a long way away. How can they compete?"

The official was becoming irritated. "We shouldn't talk about things that haven't happened yet," he said. "We need to keep calm. The whole situation will probably be sorted out soon enough. The roads will reopen."

"Says who?" a man called out.

"We're finished," said the man with horn-rimmed glasses. "The Russians have got us. We're finished."

The following day, when Stoffi came back to the flat, he had managed to buy half a large cured sausage and a loaf of crusty bread. They shared this, adding to the feast a piece of cheese that Ubi had bought from a woman on a tram – a mobile black marketeer selling her goods between stops.

Stoffi had news. He was an electrician and his job was at Templehof airport, which meant that his finger was on the pulse. "They're going to do it," he said. "They've already started."

"There are so many rumours," Ubi sighed. "How can one tell?"

Stoffi shook his head. "No, this is true. This is happening. They're going to airlift everything in. The Russians can't close the air corridors."

Ubi looked doubtful. "Everything?"

"Yes," said Stoffi. "Everything the city needs." He told Ubi that his boss at the airport had been briefed. They would be busy, he said, because the planes would be coming in non-stop.

Ubi said that he thought it would be impossible. "There are too many people," he said. "Think of the amount of food you'd have to bring in. Think of it."

"A lot," agreed Stoffi. "But then the Americans have lots of planes. And the British too."

"And coal," said Ubi. "You can't fly electricity in."

"Coal too," said Ubi. "My boss said it would be everything – including fuel."

It seemed impossible, but Stoffi assured Ubi that the planes were already coming in. "Tomorrow," he said. "Come to Templehof tomorrow. Come and see for yourself."

"I need to think about getting back," said Ubi. "I need to go home."

Stoffi laughed. "Too late, Ubi," he said. "The roads, the railway – they're not going to open them. We're surrounded by Russia now. And that means you're in Berlin, I'm afraid, until . . . until all this ends."

Over the next few days, Ubi realised that Stoffi was right, and he was trapped: travel would be impossible, particularly with an undocumented three-year-old boy. He would wait it out; the blockade could not last forever, people said, and the Russians would soon realise how unpopular they were making themselves. Stoffi shook his head. "You don't know these people," he said. "They don't think like us."

Ubi wrote to Ilse; mail was still getting through by air, although it took some days to be dispatched, and was sporadic. He told her that he would stay in Berlin for the time being, but would return when everything died down. Stoffi had said that he could get him a job at Templehof airport unloading planes. Flights were coming in now every few minutes, as the airlift began in earnest. People were needed to unload aircraft after they landed; the work was reasonably well paid and food was provided at the end of each shift. There were worse ways, he said, of spending what would be, he felt, the short days of a crisis that would surely blow over soon enough.

"I look forward so much to seeing you again," he wrote at the end of the letter. "I miss you more than I can say, my dearest one, my love."

He looked at the sentence he had just written. He had not told her that before; he had not told her that he was in love with her, not in so many words. *I am no Goethe*, he thought. But now he said it, and something deep within him shifted: an emotional barrier that had been in place ever since the day he donned a uniform; a barrier that had stood between him and the outside world, a barrier designed to show others how strong and self-sufficient he was. It was the same, he thought, with so many men, with all the soldiers of the world perhaps, who were made to seem what in reality they just were not.

THREE

IN FRIENDSHIP'S HANDS

21

After their brief honeymoon, Mike returned to duty at the airfield and Val went back to work on the farm. Archie had pretended not to notice her pregnancy, but now, with a certain embarrassment, he asked her about her plans.

"Your baby," he said, looking anywhere but at the obvious bulge. "He'll be an American, I suppose. Now that you . . ."

She smiled. "His dad is, so, I suppose he'll be too. I'm not sure how these things work."

Archie nodded. "And you too – you'll be going over there?"

"Eventually."

"With the baby?"

"Well, I'd hardly leave him here, would I?"

He smiled. "Of course. I wasn't thinking." He paused. "Which means you won't be working here much longer."

She told him that she would work for a couple of months longer. She could do most things, but would probably avoid the heavier tasks, if he did not mind. "Then I'll leave and wait for the baby."

"And what if they send your husband away?" asked Archie. "They won't be here forever, what with the war ending, and all that. You don't need all those planes now that them Germans have given up, do you?"

"We'll see," said Val. "Mike says that they have to keep the planes somewhere, and he thinks they'll probably keep his people here for a while. He said they might have to go to Germany itself."

Archie shook his head. "They don't want to go over there,"

he said. "Bad place, that. And bombed to pieces, judging from the pictures in the paper."

Something was still clearly bothering him, and he looked at her enquiringly. "He's still over at the base," he ventured, "but you're at your aunt's place. Haven't they got housing for married couples?"

She saw him blush.

"No," she said. "They haven't. Not at the base. But we have a room at my aunt's, and he can spend weekends with me there. We get by."

He quickly changed the subject. They would need to attend to the hens, he said. The fox had somehow found his way into the coop the previous night and taken the cockerel and two of his spouses. "More than he could eat," Archie said, shaking his head. "I'm going to get my hands on that fellow one of these days."

She settled back into her routine. Archie was careful about giving her only light work, and he also insisted that she go home early each day. "You have to rest," he said. "In your condition."

She had been concerned about Willy. She had been worried that he would be possessive, and that he would resent Mike's return, but her fears proved unfounded. On the first occasion that Mike stayed overnight, Willy was quiet over dinner and she thought that it was through resentment. But when Mike addressed a few remarks to him – asking him whether he had ever flown – this brought forth a torrent of questions. What happened if one of your engines stopped – did the other keep the plane in the sky? What would happen if a wheel hit a rock on the runway? Could a plane fly upside down?

Mike answered his questions patiently, and with good

humour. He had seen enough of Willy in the past to know that even if he found it difficult to deal with things that were a bit complicated he was still kind, and loyal, and could hold down a job as long as it was not too demanding. He understood all that, he assured Val. "We had a guy like that in the store," he told her. "He swept the floor and stacked the shelves, although he sometimes put things in the wrong place. His life's ambition was to be one of the sheriff's deputies – he used to wear a badge he'd picked up for a dime, but of course he could never be the real thing."

Val thought this was sad. "To want to be something that you can never be – that seems sad to me."

"And yet that's what life is like for a lot of folks," said Mike. "Not everybody has our luck."

She had not thought of it as luck, but now that he spoke of it in those terms, she could see that this was what it was. It had been luck that had brought them together, when they had been born into such different worlds. It was as a result of luck that his plane had come down on a field rather than a wood. It was luck that those Dutch people had hidden him, and it was luck that that German soldier had decided to do what he did. Everything was reducible to luck – right back to being born, and the circumstances in which that took place.

But could you ever do anything about your luck, or was it an immutable hand of cards, dealt out once and to be played throughout life, with no possibility of change? She had sometimes thought about that. People said that you got the luck you deserved; that if you behaved selfishly or cruelly, you would get the luck that came with such behaviour – and that, of course, was bad luck.

Mike's luck had held out, she thought. So many fliers had not come back; he had told her about the melancholy duty of clearing out a friend's locker – as they had done with his, when they thought he had died in the crash. That duty was one that cropped up time and time again, but was every bit as hard the fourth or fifth time as the first.

Although they were married, she felt that she had no more than a tenuous hold on him. He belonged to the air force, it seemed, rather more than he belonged to her. If it was the air force's will that he should be sent somewhere, then what she felt about that counted for nothing. And so when he came to Annie's house one evening and told her that there was something he wanted to discuss with her in the village pub, she knew that this would be the news she was dreading – that of his posting.

Her hands shook as she took the small glass of cider he had bought her. He noticed; he was concerned that she was still working on Archie's farm and would have preferred her to rest. She had said that it was better to remain active; that a baby thrived if its mother still did the things she normally did.

"Are you worried about something?" he asked.

She took a sip of the cider, savouring its sweetness. "About you," she said. "I know what you're going to tell me."

She could tell from his expression it was not going to be good news.

"I'm going to Germany," he said. "I'm going to be flying transport planes. C-47s. They're really just military versions of DC-3s."

She looked at him blankly. She knew nothing of planes, although she could recognise the sort he flew.

"There's a base at Wiesbaden," Mike went on. "We took it over from the Germans. I'm going to be there."

She stared into her cider. *I'm* going to be there. *I'm* . . .

"And us?" she asked.

He bit his lip. "We'll be fine."

"But you'll . . ."

"I have to be over there, yes, and at the moment they won't let us take wives." He paused, and reached for her hand. "In the future, maybe. In fact, definitely: the air force doesn't like to split families."

"Then why . . ."

He cut her short. "Some posts are unaccompanied. It's just the way they are. They aren't sending me to Hawaii – it's to a country we've just been at war with. It's different."

"Couldn't you ask to go to Hawaii?"

He laughed. "Everybody wants to go to Hawaii. That's what Hawaii is for – it's a reward."

"Or even California? What about California?"

He shook his head. "I have to go where I'm sent. It won't be forever. Maybe you'll be able to come over next year. Who knows?"

There was something else he wanted to discuss with her. "You could be sent to the States, you know. They can arrange that. You don't have to stay here."

She had not expected this. "Without you?"

"Yes. You'd get housing on a base, maybe." He was trying to sound optimistic. "Or you can go to my mom and dad. In fact, that would be much easier."

"In Muncie, Indiana?"

He smiled. "Yes, in Muncie, Indiana. You've always wanted

to go there. You said . . ."

"But that was with you. I don't want to go there by myself."

He had spilled some of his beer on the table, and now he traced a pattern in it with a finger. "They'd look after you," he said. "And the baby too."

"But I don't know them. I'd be a stranger."

"You wouldn't. You'd be my wife. That's not a stranger."

She shook her head. "And it'd be different, wouldn't it? With the baby and everything. Even some of the words – you call nappies diapers, don't you?"

"That's not a problem, surely."

She was struggling with tears. "It could be for me."

He took her hand again. "All right, all right." He sounded defeated, and she felt a pang of guilt. After what he had gone through, she should not make it harder for him than it was. "You stay here. Have the baby at your aunt's place. We'll be together later, but in the meantime . . ." He tried again to appear positive. "In the meantime, you'll be comfortable here with your aunt and with Willy. And there's Peter Woodhouse. He can stay with you, of course."

She hesitated, but finally decided. "He's your dog now. Take him to Germany with you. He's an American dog."

He grinned. "Do dogs think like that? Do they care about these things? British dogs, American dogs . . . it's all the same to them."

She smiled – for the first time that evening, and he pressed her hand in his, encouraging her. "Probably is," she said. "But still. He's used to you. You take him."

He looked thoughtful and almost agreed. But then he shook his head and explained that it would be better for him to stay.

"This base is all right," he said. "But who knows what it'll be like over there. No, this is his place. This country. This place probably smells right to him – you know how dogs are with their smells."

She did not argue. "He could go back to the farm – to Archie. He'll look after him."

"The best thing for him," said Mike.

She felt the baby kick, and she took his hand and placed it on her stomach. He thought about what she had said about Peter Woodhouse. American babies, British babies . . . even German babies . . . They were all the same. Things went wrong only after they were born.

He wanted to say something, but no words came. *Being close to death can make us look at the world with different eyes . . .* It was what the chaplain at the base had said to him on his return. He was referring to the crash, of course, but it had occurred to Mike that the observation could be interpreted more widely; given that the human lifespan was so short, it might apply throughout life. We were always close to death, young or old: we did not have all that long. He had been about to say something to that effect, but he stopped himself; he had heard that the chaplain liked nothing more than a theological discussion, and had been known to detain a busy man for over an hour in the exploration of some abstruse point. On one famous occasion he had even held up a mission –delaying the departure of avenging angels by almost ten minutes.

22

He was already in Wiesbaden when the baby arrived. Annie went to the base to hand over the letter that one of the air force clerks had promised to get delivered within two or three days – unlike the normal post, which could take weeks to reach an overseas address. She wrote: *Your baby son has arrived safely. I am writing to tell you this because Val is still in the hospital and they don't want her to do anything very much just yet. We'll send a photograph as soon as we can arrange one, but Val said: "Tell Mike that he looks just like him." He took a long time to arrive – it wasn't easy for her, labour being that long and all, but he's here now, safe and sound, and as strong and as hungry as can be. One of the nurses says that American babies are all like that – all very strong – and maybe she's right. Val sends you her dearest love. She says to tell you that she thinks of you all the time, and that she knows you will love your new little Thomas Barnes Rogers the moment you see him, which she hopes will be very soon. She sends you all her love and asks you not to worry about anything – she has everything she needs and is very happy.*

It was five days before she was allowed home, and then only on the strength of a promise from Annie that she would enforce bed rest for a further week. She had lost more blood than they would have liked, but gradually her strength returned. Thomas Barnes Rogers – "such an impressive name for a baby" said Annie – or Tommy, as he had already become, was bundled up in ancient lace baby clothes from Annie's attic and wheeled about in a carriage pram that the midwife had summoned up from somewhere. Willy doted on the new arrival, and would talk of nothing else over meals. Was Tommy sleeping enough? Should the district nurse be asked to come to listen to his chest? Was the house warm enough for him? Small babies did not like draughts – they could get croup from them, he had been told. You could never be too careful when they were that small.

"Calm down, Willy," said Annie. "Babies are tough little things – especially large babies like this one. If he gets his milk regularly and the air in his room is kept warm, he'll thrive all right, you mark my words."

"Auntie's right," said Val. "You don't want to wrap babies up too much. Their skin needs air on it. Nurse said that herself. That's exactly what she said."

"I know a thing or two," said Willy resentfully. "I've read them books too."

'Of course you have, Willy," said Annie. "And Tommy will be fine, with you and Val looking after him, and the whole village behind him, egging him on. He's going to grow into a fine little boy before any of us knows it."

There were extra rations for a nursing mother, and Archie made sure that there was no shortage of eggs, butter and cream. "Cream is what you need," he said to Val, standing awkwardly at the door of her room when he came to visit, fingering the brim of his cap, embarrassed to enter this room of mother and baby equipment, of bottles and towels, and the soft, slightly sour-milk smell of a tiny infant. "I can get you plenty of cream now."

She asked him what he thought of the baby. He edged into the room and peered into the cradle. "He's a proper healthy nipper," he said. "Got your eyes, I think."

She laughed. "That's what Willy thinks too."

"And when will they let your fellow come back?"

She sighed. "I don't know, Archie. I'll go over there, I think, once everything's sorted out. There's not much housing yet – even for officers."

He raised an eyebrow. "You told me that before. I thought they always looked after officers. There are always houses for officers."

"Not over there there's not."

Archie nodded. "You'll see him soon enough, I expect." He moved away from the cradle. "And young fellow-my-lad over there will keep you busy meanwhile."

She enquired about the farm; was he coping now that she was no longer working? He replied that he was, but that there were things he was having to give up. There would be no turnips next year, he thought, but the field he normally grew them in could do with a rest anyway.

"And Willy?" he said, looking over his shoulder towards the kitchen, where Willy and Annie could be heard conversing. "Do you think he might want to come and work at my place?"

"You could ask him. I don't see why not."

Archie looked thoughtful. "He's a good boy, that."

Val agreed; and she was not just saying that. Willy was a good boy, even if he was impetuous at times and even if he did go on and on about some subjects – babies currently, but that would change as something else attracted his attention.

Willy's enthusiasm for Tommy proved not to be a passing phase. Not only did he continue to talk incessantly about him – thoughts of the baby occupying his every waking moment – but he proved to be a staunch ally in the watches of the night,

IN FRIENDSHIP'S HANDS   183

when Tommy awoke to be fed and he would make tea for Val, averting his eyes if he brought it to her as she was feeding the baby. Then he would wait outside the door until she called him back in, when he would take Tommy in his arms and rock him, murmuring in the low voice that the baby seemed to find calming. Val watched, and thought of how nobody would ever have dreamed that Willy would show qualities like this, would behave like the most devoted of fathers.

She had spoken to him about Archie, and had been surprised by Willy's easy acceptance of the suggestion that he should leave the farm he was on.

"That would be all right with me," he said. "I like Archie."

"He's a nice man to work for," said Val. "He never asks you to do too much. He's kind."

Willy nodded. "And it'll be easier for me to look after Tommy if I work there," he said. "Closer, you see. I can get back here quicker."

She was silent. The attachment was deeper than she had imagined.

She tried to be gentle. "Of course, Tommy and I are going to have to go one of these days, Willy. Not now, mind, but maybe . . . well, maybe in a few months' time." She paused. "Mike will be counting the days until he sees his boy for the first time."

Willy looked away. "I know that," he said.

The next day an idea occurred to her. The vicar visited and spoke to her about the christening. "Have you discussed baptism with the father?" he asked, searching his memory for the name. He had married them, after all, and he did try to remember all the names, but it was difficult.

"Mike," she said. "No, I haven't spoken to him, but he'll not mind. I can write to him."

The vicar said he thought this was the thing to do. "I'm a great believer in early baptism," he said. "As early as possible, I always say."

She smiled. The vicar always said *I always say*; round and round in a circle, *I always say I always say* . . .

"And godparents?" he asked.

She had given the matter no thought, but that did not stop her replying. "Willy, I think."

The vicar inclined his head. "He'll be very proud of that, I suspect."

"He will be."

"And the others? It's normal for a boy to have two godfathers and one godmother. And the other way round, *mutatis mutandis*." He smiled apologetically.

"Is that Latin?"

He laughed. "Yes, it is. I know I shouldn't quote Latin – people don't always like it – but somehow . . ."

She said, smiling, "We all do things we shouldn't do. Quoting Latin is not the worst thing you could do."

"The other godparents?"

The answer came just as easily as it had with Willy. "There's Archie Wilkinson up at the farm. You know him?"

"A good man," said the vicar.

She looked at the vicar's shoes. They had been good shoes once, she thought, well made black shoes in a style she had seen described as Oxfords. But now there were cracks in the leather, like lines across a furrowed brow. Of course, shoes had needed coupons for a long time, and now they were reduced to only three a week, to cover everything. It was worse than in

wartime, because now they had to clothe all those people in
Germany who had nothing but the rags they stood up in. They
started it, and it was their fault, she thought, but they were
still people, and a lot of them were women and children who
presumably had not wanted war in the first place; not really,
even if there were those photographs showing them waving
flags and saluting Hitler just like the men.

"And my aunt," she said. "She'd love to be godmother."

"I'm sure she would," said the vicar. "But will you be
discussing it with . . . with . . ."

"Mike."

"Yes, Mike. Ask the father, I always say, even if he's not there.
He should be asked."

She said she would do that, and she wrote about it in her next
letter. He wrote back, *Whatever you want, my darling. Everything
for you. You're the one! Everything.*

Now she could ask Willy, and the others too. But speaking to
Willy, she felt, was the most important.

He listened attentively, nodding his head as she spoke. Then,
when she had finished, he said, "Godfather?"

"Yes. The vicar holds a service. We all go – even Tommy. And
the vicar splashes him with water . . . well, not actually splashes,
just pours a little over his head." She paused; sometimes it was
difficult to work out just what Willy knew. "You must have
seen it, Willy."

"Of course I've seen it," he said. "Lots of times, down at the
church."

"Well, there you are. You know all about it."

He looked thoughtful. "Godfather? That's like . . . like being
a father, sort of, when the father isn't there? Like that?"

She hesitated. "Well, it's not quite that. It's not quite like being the father. That's different, you see. A father's . . ."

He cut her short. "I know that." He gave her a reproachful look. He was sensitive to being thought not to know things; if people thought that he knew nothing, they were wrong. Often, they were the ones who failed to grasp something that he knew perfectly well. How animals felt, for instance, or what the clouds meant for the weather ahead, or the various types of bird nest, or what was wrong with the country. And here was Val implying that he did not know what godfathers were for. "Of course, I know that. But when the father's away somewhere, or dead, or something, then you still have the godfather, don't you?"

"You could put it like that. But the main thing is that the godfather's kind to the baby. He remembers birthdays – that sort of thing."

Willy grinned. "I can do that," he said.

"Of course you can, Willy."

The vicar's cracked shoes projected from under his white cassock, the hem of which was frayed, as everything was after five years of war and the shortages that war brought. There was even a smell to parsimony, some said: a thin, musty smell of things used beyond their natural life, of materials patched up, cobbled together, persuaded to do whatever it was they did well after they should have been retired. And it was true of people too – with both young men and young women in uniform, those left behind to do the day-to-day jobs seemed tired, overworked, made to carry on with their duties well after they should have been pensioned off. And now the vicar looked up at his small congregation and took a deep breath, as if summoning up for the task ahead what little energy he had left.

Val sat in the front pew, flanked by Annie and Willy, with Archie, stiff in his ancient suit, on the other side of Willy. The vicar closed his eyes as he spoke, only opening them occasionally to look out on the heads of those in the pews: the familiar words required no reading; he had uttered them countless times before. At first Val only half listened, being preoccupied with Tommy, who was awake but silent in her arms, all but completely covered in the christening robe Annie had made for him from scraps of white cotton and lace. But then she found herself following the vicar's words, drawn in by the poetry of the liturgy.

"Beloved," he said, and Val thought, *That's us*; and he continued, "you hear in this Gospel the words of our Saviour Christ, that he commanded the children to be brought unto him . . . You perceive how by his outward gesture and deed he declared his goodwill toward them; for he embraced them in his arms, he laid his hands upon them, and blessed them. Doubt not therefore, but earnestly believe, that he will likewise favourably receive this present infant; that he will embrace him with the arms of his mercy . . ."

Val did not think that God existed, but she liked the idea that he was there, even if it was no more than a fond hope – that thing that people called faith. Even the vicar, she thought, must have his doubts, because if God did exist, then why had he let all those people die in the war; all those innocent people herded into those camps and murdered; all those besieged Russians starving to death, eating rats to keep alive; all those children who died under the rain of bombs? Why did he allow all that when by one movement of his finger he could have obliterated the Nazis and their works, stopped the slaughter and the suffering?

But now the vicar held the little bundle in his arms and reached for a tarnished silver spoon on the edge of the font. He had said that the water would be warm – as warm as the River Jordan, he smilingly assured her; and he sprinkled a few drops on Tommy's forehead. The child's eyes opened, surprised, unfocused, but he did not cry, and he was handed back to her as she struggled to keep from crying herself. She was thinking of Mike, who would have been so proud at this moment, and would have put his arm around her, she thought. She missed him so painfully. It was an insistent, raw ache of longing, assuaged from time to time by the joy of having Tommy. But as the weeks of separation drew into months, she found it increasingly hard to remember what the man she had married had been like. Even his face was becoming blurred in her memory now; their times together remembered, but in such a way as to make her ask herself whether she was recalling them correctly. What did his voice sound like? What did he say to her when he spoke about Indiana and the life he had led there? What did he whisper to her in their moments of intimacy?

Her dreams began to disturb her. He appeared in some of them, but it was only to tell her that he had found somebody else, or to reveal that he was actually dead and they had not got round to telling her yet, and he was sorry that she was the last to hear. In her dreams she always said that it did not matter, that she still loved him, but for some reason when she tried to address him he was not there, but was in a unfamiliar place

IN FRIENDSHIP'S HANDS   189

somewhere else, a place that was something like the air force base but with no planes, just tractors. As places do in dreams, it had a fluid identity; it was a farm, and then it was not a farm but the village, and then part of a landscape that she did not recognise but that must have been Muncie, Indiana.

He came back on leave when Tommy was four months old, and again five months later. They went to Cornwall, where they had spent their honeymoon, and stayed for a week in a boarding house where the food was cold and generally unpalatable. The woman who ran it offered to babysit, and they went to the local cinema, the Electric Palace. After the film, they called in at a pub where a pianist played "The White Cliffs of Dover" and everybody started to sing. Looks were exchanged – looks of relief, coupled with nostalgia. A man, a perfect stranger, bought Mike a drink, saying, "In case people haven't said thank you." Mike said, "We did it together," and the man nodded, but said nothing further.

Eventually, on another long leave, he told her that he was likely to be in Germany for some time yet. "You'll have to come," he said. "There's somebody on the base who can arrange a place for us now. Nothing special, but it'll be a roof over our heads."

"When?" she asked.

"Next week," he said. Then he added, "You'll have to tell Willy as tactfully as you can – you can see how attached he's become to Tommy."

She sighed. "He lives for him." It was true, she thought. And then there was the unspoken fear that, for Tommy, Willy was his father. Mike was a stranger to the boy, who was now almost two.

Mike shrugged. "I guess he'll get used to it."

"He will. He'll be sad, though."

He said that he thought that sadness, mostly, never lasted very long. "It's not the way people are made," he said. "We're made to get moving, to get on with the next thing. To look to the future."

He was right, she thought, but it would still be hard for Willy, who had no next thing, at least as far as she could see.

She broke the news of her departure to Willy as gently as she could. For a few moments he was silent; then he looked away, avoiding her eyes.

"I'm sure I'll be back," she said. "From time to time. Quite often, in fact."

He glanced at her quickly, and then his gaze slid away once more.

"You won't," he muttered.

"Willy!" she exclaimed. "Don't be like that. I wouldn't tell you I'd be coming back if I wasn't going to. Of course I'll come back and see you and Annie – and Peter Woodhouse. To see everybody, in fact."

His face was full of reproach. "No, you won't. You may think you will, but you'll be far away, won't you? Over in Germany, and then what? That place in America? That Indiana? You won't come back from there – it's too far."

He was right, of course, and she realised it. Yet she had no stomach for a real leave-taking – there had been so many of those in the war years, when goodbye had meant goodbye as never before.

"I'll do my best," she said. "And I'll write to you."

She suddenly became aware that Willy was crying. She put her arms about him, but he tried to push her away, as a child avoiding an embrace might do. She wanted to cry too; for everything, for the war, for Willy's loneliness, for the ache that separation or the prospect of separation brought with it. She wanted to cry for the world that seemed to have come to such an abrupt end: the world of England before the war, when everything had seemed so secure. Now England itself seemed to be built on shaky foundations. England was changing into something else – a country where everything had been shaken up and spilled out in a quite other pattern from that which she had been used to. They had known what they were fighting for, but now that they had it, it seemed to be something quite different.

"I wish you wouldn't cry, Willy," she said. "You're going to be fine."

He wiped at his eyes clumsily. "What about Tommy?" he asked.

"Tommy will write too. And I'll send you photographs."

It occurred to her that Willy was hoping for a different response – that Tommy could somehow be left behind.

"He has to be with his father," she added quickly. "You do see that, don't you?"

With a supreme effort, Willy nodded. "I hope he'll be all right," he said. 'Over there in Germany . . .'"

He left the sentence unfinished.

"He'll be well looked after. The US Air Force has schools. Swimming pools, playgrounds – everything."

He wiped his eyes again. "When he's bigger he could come and visit the farm," he said. "He could help me and Archie."

She seized at this. "Of course he could. That's a lovely idea, Willy."

"He could pick plums," Willy went on. "Small fellow like that can climb up on the branches without breaking them. He could reach the plums."

"Yes," said Val. "He could do that all right, Willy – when he's bigger."

One of the other wives in Wiesbaden, the wife of a major, took her out for coffee shortly after she arrived and asked her about her life before she was married. "I'm just curious, you see. A lot of the men married, didn't they? I often wonder what it's been like for their wives – coming from somewhere different and then being taken back to the States where they have no family, you know. It can't be easy."

Val told her about being a land girl. She told her about meeting Mike and the dances at the base.

The major's wife smiled. "I always knew I was going to marry Bill. From about sixteen, I think." She paused. "I don't think he knew, though."

They both laughed.

"And now?" said the major's wife. "What about now?"

"I'm happy. We're together. And that's the important thing."

"Of course it is."

"So I feel that my life – our life, I suppose – is just starting."

This brought a nod of the head. "And there's your little boy – a cute little guy. You're lucky."

"Yes. I know that."

"But," said the major's wife. "But . . ."

"But what?"

"The Russians. Berlin. These extra duties. Bill says . . ."

Val waited.

"Bill says we're in for a long haul. They're going to have to fly everything in – food, coal, the whole lot. The British, ourselves – everyone's going to have to keep them alive. He says he can't see how we can do it." She sighed. "Was life meant to be like this, do you think? I mean, when you think about what we really want – to find somebody, fall in love, get married and so on. Have kids. Enjoy ourselves. And what do we get instead? World War Two. The Russians. Berlin."

"Oh well . . ."

The major's wife smiled. "You English people," she said. "I don't get you. You say things like *oh well* and then you carry on as if nothing ever happened."

"Do we have any choice?"

"Maybe not."

"So we may as well say *oh well*."

"Maybe."

Later, when Mike came off duty, he told her that he was going to have to go to a different base for emergency duties. She and Tommy were to stay where they were.

"Berlin?" she asked. The papers had been full of the news of the blockade.

He nodded. "I'm going to be flying non-stop, more or less. Every pilot we have."

He moved forward to embrace her, and she felt that familiar feeling of longing that had never once gone away when she was in his presence. She wanted the moment to be frozen; she wanted to be with him, exclusively and alone, with nothing else around them. She wanted to hold him to her and not to let him go from her. Ever. Ever.

He drew back, and looked at her fondly. "Sometimes," he said, "the world has other plans for people, doesn't it? But the people themselves . . . the people . . ."

"Yes?"

"The people themselves have to hold onto their own plans . . . and hope that they get the chance to carry them out."

They were standing in the kitchen. She took his hand. She held it gently: a hand that guided planes; a human hand. "Please be careful."

He smiled at her. "I'll take care. I always do."

"But especially careful. More careful than ever before."

He put a finger against her lips, as much to silence as to reassure her. "Yes," he said. "Don't worry."

23

Returned to Archie's farm, Peter Woodhouse became once more a farm dog, housed in the old removers' crate marked with the stencilled legend *Peter Woodhouse* on the side. Archie had been pleased by his return, as was Willy, who now worked six days a week on the tasks that the older farmer was beginning to find more difficult, with his troublesome hip and his increasing breathlessness. The doctor had said that Archie should retire altogether; his remaining years, he urged, would be better spent – and more numerous – were he to hang up his boots and sit in the warmth of the farmhouse kitchen.

"You've got that young fellow helping you," the doctor said. "There's plenty of hard work in him and you've done your bit." He spoke with conviction, but without much hope that his advice would be heeded; in his experience, farmers rarely retired, tending to die on the job. It was what they wanted, he supposed, although he could still spell it out to them.

"You won't last all that long," he said, "if you don't take things easily. That chest of yours . . ."

"Lasted me until now," said Archie. "Still got the puff to keep me going."

"Yes, but . . ." The doctor sighed.

"When I go, I go," said Archie. "Same as with animals. They know when it's time. They just keep going until the time comes, and then they go."

Peter Woodhouse, of course, was no longer a young dog. Like his owner, he appeared to have something wrong with a hip, and walked with a marked limp. This did not stop him trying to keep up with Willy when he drove the tractor, but he could not carry on for long, and soon fell panting by the wayside, watching Willy disappear down the farm lane. For the most part, he lay in his kennel, or immediately in front of it, where there was a large paving stone that warmed with the sun. On the rare occasions when visitors arrived in the farmyard, he would give a few desultory barks, and then sidle up to them in a show of unqualified affection. "He's no guard dog, that one," said Archie.

Willy defended Peter. "Doesn't mean he isn't brave," he said. "He went up with them in those planes of theirs. He's seen action – which is more than most dogs can claim."

Archie smiled. "Yes. Good pilot, they say."

He had a new collar, given him by the airmen at the base when he left. Inscribed on it, burned into the leather with the tip of a soldering iron, was *The Good Pilot Peter Woodhouse*. A visitor noticed this – a reporter from the local weekly who was doing an article on rights-of-way through farms. He asked about its meaning, and Archie explained about the dog's time as a US Air Force mascot.

"You serious?" asked the reporter.

"Yes, of course. They took him up with them."

The reporter's incredulity grew. "In their planes? Over to Germany?"

"So I've been told," said Archie. "Apparently, he liked flying."

The reporter whistled. "What a story," he muttered.

A photographer came to take a picture of Peter Woodhouse in front of his kennel. Then he took a shot of the collar and its inscription. In due course an article appeared on the front page of the weekly newspaper published in the nearby market town.

The Good Pilot Peter Woodhouse, it was headed, with the sub-heading *Brave dog helps fliers on wartime missions.* There was a picture of Sergeant Lisowski, whom the paper had approached for comment. "He was given an honourable discharge," the sergeant said. "He did his bit."

Willy beamed with pleasure when he saw the paper. He bought every copy for sale in the post office, cut out the article, and sent one off to Val in Germany. She sent a postcard back on which she had written: *Our Peter Woodhouse! The hero!*

Annie was more reserved. "I'm not sure that Peter Woodhouse needs to be in the papers," she said. "What if that Ted Butters sees it? He can read, you know, same as anyone else."

Willy shook his head. "Ted Butters wouldn't dare do anything."

Annie looked dubious. "I'd put nothing past him," she said.

They were looking at the tractor, which was misfiring and emitting white smoke.

"The injectors," said Archie. "Do you know about those, Willy?"

Willy nodded, but looked blank at the same time.

Archie showed him. There were so many things that Willy knew nothing about, but the farmer had found him to be a quick learner, in spite of everything. If you engaged his attention, he could pick things up, and you would not know, then, that he was slow. Now Archie showed him how to remove the exhaust manifold so that they could work out which cylinder was pumping out white smoke from unburnt fuel.

"There," said Archie. "You see over there? That's the culprit."

"Can we fix it?" asked Willy.

Archie did not reply. A small brown van was making its way up the lane towards the farmyard, and Archie was gazing at it. "That's Ted Butters," he muttered.

They watched as Ted Butters drew to a halt at the farmyard gate. He got out of the van, opened the gate, and then drove through, omitting to close it again behind him.

"Hey!" shouted Archie. "The gate. You didn't close the gate. We've got livestock . . ."

Ted Butters ignored him.

"You!" he said, pointing at Willy. "Where's my dog?"

Archie felt Willy stiffen and bristle. He put a restraining hand on the young man's arm. "Listen to me, Butters," he began. "You come on my land, you talk to me – understand?"

Ted Butters turned to face Archie. "Very well," he said. "I've got the same question for you – where's my dog?"

"He ain't your dog any more, Butters," said Archie firmly. "You mistreated him. You know you did. He left you."

Ted Butters snorted with anger. "You stole him, more likely. That dog cost six quid, and you stole him."

Willy now joined in. "He left you," he said. "He ran away."

Ted Butters looked at him contemptuously. "Liar," he said. "Not that you'll know the meaning of the word."

Willy flushed. "I know what it means."

Ted Butters rolled his eyes. "That's a good one," he said. He took a few steps forward to get a better view of the farmyard. He noticed Peter Woodhouse's kennel, and the dog lying down, half inside, half outside.

"So what's that over there?" he sneered.

He walked purposively over towards the kennel. Archie

hobbled after him.

"You leave that dog alone, Butters," Archie shouted.

Ted Butters did not turn round, but began to walk more quickly towards the kennel. As he approached it, Peter Woodhouse stirred, and then sat up. He sniffed at the air, and fixed his gaze on the angry farmer.

Ted Butters was now a few paces away. He called out to the dog, who rose to his feet, and began to growl. Butters looked about and spotted a stone on the ground. He bent down to pick this up, and made a gesture as if throwing it at the dog. "Don't you growl at me, my lad," he muttered.

The action of picking up the stone was enough. Deep in his memory, Peter Woodhouse recognised the smell of the man who had tormented and beaten him. Now, with almost no hesitation, he lurched forward, baring his teeth. Ted Butters stopped in his tracks, and then threw the stone, the missile hitting the dog on the top of his head with a dull thud. For a moment, Peter Woodhouse seemed to topple, but he soon righted himself and his eyes flashed with hatred. Hurling himself forward with something midway between a yelp and a growl, he charged at Ted Butters, sinking his teeth into the man's leg and then momentarily disengaging before latching onto his flailing arm.

Willy rushed forward and seized Peter Woodhouse by the collar, wrenching him bodily off his victim. Ted Butters, freed of the dog, aimed a kick at Peter's flank but missed, losing his balance as a result, and falling heavily to the ground. Archie, now at the fallen farmer's side, bent down to help him to his feet.

Once upright, Ted Butters brushed away Archie's hand.

"That dog's dead," he spat out. "He'll be shot. I'm going straight to Bill Edwards."

"You asked for it," said Willy, his voice high with indignation. 'You threw a stone at him. What do you expect a dog to do?"

"He'll be shot," replied Ted Butters, wincing with pain. "The police shoot dogs that attack people. You know that as well as I do."

"Not if they're just defending themselves," countered Archie. "There's a difference."

"I'll shoot him myself," said Ted.

Archie stepped forward. "If you come on my land with a shotgun you'll get more than you bargained for."

Ted Butters gave him a murderous look. "The police will be here," he said. "You'll see." He stormed off towards his van, and they noticed, as he went, that there was blood on his trouser leg where Peter Woodhouse had bitten him. Archie looked anxious; Ted Butters was right about dogs being shot if they attacked people. There had been a case the previous year where that was exactly what had happened; a dog had savaged a ten-year-old girl and had been shot the same afternoon by Bill Edwards. Bill had disliked doing it, but had been given instructions by the station sergeant in the nearby town, who had not been prepared to listen to any of the owners' pleas for mercy.

Willy suddenly started to run towards the retreating farmer. Archie moved to intercept him, but was too slow. Willy grabbed at Ted and jerked him back off his feet. Then he appeared to shake him, as a dog might shake a rabbit, before dropping him on the ground.

"Willy!" Archie shouted. "Let him be."

Willy stood over Ted, his face flushed with rage. "You beat that dog," he yelled. "You deserve everything you get."

Reaching Willy's side, Archie pushed him roughly away and bent down to help Ted to his feet.

"You've added assault to the charges," Ted spluttered. "Grievous bodily harm, I shouldn't wonder."

Archie glanced at Willy over his shoulder, warning him off. A small trickle of blood was emerging from Ted's right nostril, his nose having felt some of the impact of his fall.

"You brought all this on yourself, Ted," Archie muttered. "You always were like that, you know. Caused trouble wherever you went."

"You stole my dog," said Ted.

Archie shook his head. "We've been through that, Ted." He paused. A solution was dawning on him. "How much to settle?" he asked.

Ted Butters rubbed at his nose, his hand coming away bloodied. He was a farmer after all, and his farmer's instinct was coming into play. Money could sort out most issues, judiciously applied, and this might be one of them. "Fifteen quid," he said, glaring over Archie's shoulder at Willy in the background.

"Twelve pounds ten shillings," countered Archie. "He's getting on a bit now, that dog."

"Fourteen," replied Ted Butters. "And half a dozen hens – good layers."

Archie looked at Willy, who had started to walk over towards Peter Woodhouse's kennel. "All right," he said. "Fourteen quid and four hens."

24

The job that Ubi took on at Templehof involved six ten-hour shifts a week. It was unremittingly hard work, every bit as physically demanding, he thought, as working in a mine, but there were the meals, which were rich and sustaining, and there was the pride of competition, too, which made a difference. Each crew kept a note of the times it took to open the hatches of the incoming aircraft and unload the cargo onto the waiting trucks. With the planes coming down every couple of minutes, the ground operation was as slick and precise as the airlift itself. There was a room in which they could spend a few minutes recovering after each unloading, but the drone of the departing aircraft would soon merge into that of the next descending, a ceaseless background sound, like that of the waves on a shore.

Everything that the city needed was brought in this way – across the invisible air bridge that linked Berlin with the West. The Russians had closed every ground route into the city, ruthlessly strangling the three non-Soviet sectors. It would not be long, they calculated, before the task of keeping hundreds of thousands of people alive would prove just too much, even with the might of the Americans behind it. How could you bring in enough food to feed that many people day after day? You could not. How could you bring in sufficient coal to generate a whole city's power? You could not.

Many of those who did the unloading were volunteers, working for the free meals alone; some, like Ubi, who was given charge of a crew, were paid. Some of the money he earned went to Stoffi as rent for the floor that was his bed;

some of it went to the widow, for Klaus. His own needs were small enough, and he was used now to poverty and paucity.

He wrote every other day to Ilse, even when he was tired at the end of a gruelling shift, his ears ringing with the sound of the aircraft engines. In her replies, she sent him long accounts of the doings of the British officers. There was the story of the junior maid in the hotel, who had taken up with one of the officers, and now had confessed to being pregnant. There was the story of the officer who had taken an interest in the *Motodrom*. He had managed to get hold of some paint from somewhere and had offered to paint it for her. She had accepted, but was worried that they would take it away from her. *They can requisition things they need*, she wrote. *What if they decide the occupying forces need a* Motodrom? She was fond of it, in a curious way, and was even wondering whether it might be rescued as a paying attraction. A local mechanic had been to see her about it. He and a friend were keen to disassemble it and move it to a field on the edge of town. People would pay to come and watch it being ridden. They would charge admission and then would split the proceeds with her. What should she do about that? Should she accept?

He wrote back and told her about his airlift duties. *I am black from unloading coal*, he said. *Then the next plane comes in and it's carrying sacks of flour. So I become white. Now, your* Motodrom: *yes, you should let other people use it, but you mustn't give it away. A* Motodrom *is an unusual thing, and you're lucky to have it. I can help you when I come back. I can help you run it and perhaps we can let the mechanic be the rider, if that's what he wants.*

She responded that the officer had finished the painting. She had offered to pay him something, but this had just caused surprise, and even offence. He had looked at her sideways; did she not understand who they were? She was a German civilian, one of the vanquished, and he was one of the conquerors. The offence might have been less had he been one of the men, but he was an officer. She said that he had bitten his lip and declined her offer in a voice that sounded as if he were being strangled. *They are very proud men*, she wrote. And then added, *Not that we should accuse others of being proud.* He reread that sentence, and knew that she was right. There was something very deep in the soul of his country that made it want to dominate; that thing, that lurking quality, was wounded now, but it would find a new way to express itself one day. He did not want that to happen; he had hated the strutting and the arrogance, but he knew that it was still there, even if bullied into submission. He had seen it in people's eyes: the glint that told him those fires were not entirely or everywhere extinguished.

Her letters were the high point of his day. When one failed to arrive, as sometimes happened during the blockade, he went back to the last one he had received, and often found that it contained new things to think about. His time now was largely filled with work, punctuated by visits to the widow and Klaus. The boy was getting used to him, and looked forward to the chocolate passed on from the American fliers. On one occasion Ubi received half a carton of cigarettes from an airman who had just been told that he was to be posted home at last, and was feeling generous. He was able to exchange that for a new pair of boy's shoes and a barely worn child's overcoat. The widow said, "I'm rationing his chocolate," but he suspected that she ate much of it herself, and had once seen traces of it about her lips. But everyone had become like that, he realised; these were still times of bare survival. The coat went missing after a few weeks and he did not believe her protestations that it had been left on a tram. He did not accuse her of trading it on the black market, but he was certain that this was what had happened.

They were unloading medical supplies. The cartons were light – bandages and pills did not weigh a great deal – and they completed their task in not much more than ten minutes. There was mail to be loaded for the return journey, but, unusually, there was no urgency. The plane required a repair, and that would take over twelve hours. The crew would be stood down for at least eight of those and could go off into the city if they wished. They went ahead with the loading, though, so that the plane would be ready for take-off the moment the repairs were finished. Every lost hour meant less cargo, and that could be translated into hunger or cold for somebody in the beleaguered city. It was while Ubi was bringing in the last of the mail sacks that the pilot emerged from the flight deck. Ubi moved to the side to let him pass, and for a moment the two men were side by side. The pilot glanced at him briefly and then stopped. He reached out to put a hand on Ubi's shoulder, and the two men looked into each other's face.

There was no doubt in the mind of either, but for a few moments nothing was said. There had been so many painful moments of recognition that people were wary. Recognition could mean denunciation and arrest; there were full dress trials that had resulted from a passing glance in the street.

"It is you, isn't it?" Mike said. "Holland?"

Ubi was silent.

"It is, isn't it?"

Mike's smile gave him the reassurance he needed. "Yes, it's me."

Mike moved forward and flung his arms round Ubi. "You protected us."

Ubi made a gesture of helplessness. "The war was over."

"It wasn't. You took a big risk. And our dog too. You saved his life." Mike released him from the hug. "And here you are," he said.

"You're speaking German," said Ubi.

Mike laughed. "I've learned. Classes at the base. I have an ear, I'm told. I picked up a bit of Dutch too . . . back then."

"So did I."

Mike gestured to the loaded mail bags. "And this is what you're doing?"

"For the time being. I want to get back to the West. I have a fiancée back there, but there's a small boy here – my sister's son. She died."

Mike lowered his eyes. "I'm sorry."

"It's difficult," said Ubi. "Papers and so on. And now the blockade."

"Ah, papers. Papers control our lives, don't they?" Mike hesitated. "I reckon I owe you."

Ubi said nothing.

Mike looked at his watch. Night and day made little difference to the working of the air bridge, but he could see that it was coming up for dinner time. "When do you finish your shift?" he asked.

"Now," said Ubi. "You were the last plane – for us, at least."

"I don't really know Berlin," said Mike. "Are there any restaurants left standing?"

Ubi nodded. "There's *Der Kleine Friedrich* not far from here. They say it's good. I've never been."

"And they have food?"

"Some."

Mike smiled as he placed a friendly hand on Ubi's shoulder. "Will you let me buy you dinner? As a thank you."

Ubi protested that Mike did not need to thank him for anything.

"I know that," said Mike. "But I want to."

"In that case, yes."

Der Kleine Friedrich was in the basement of a building that had miraculously survived the destruction round about it. The blockade had dimmed the electric light bulbs that festooned the entrance to the bar, but inside, strategically placed candles gave a nightclub air of complicity and decadence. A small band, consisting of a pianist, a violinist and a clarinettist – all emaciated and well into their sixties – made a brave attempt at cheerfulness, mixing Dixie and Weimar in a curious mish-mash of time and place.

They sat by the bar while a table was prepared for them. Ubi, who had been unable to change out of his working clothes, seemed ill at ease; Mike, in his flying jacket and boots, was insouciant, and largely indifferent to the thinly disguised condescension of the barman.

Mike asked Ubi about his experiences as a prisoner of war. He heard about Ilse and the billeted British officers. He heard about the search for his sister and for Klaus.

"It hasn't been as bad for me as it has for so many," said Ubi. "I haven't really suffered."

Mike shrugged. "Luck, I guess. We were lucky that you found us back there. It might have been very different. Some of your people . . ." He stopped.

Ubi looked down at the floor. "You can say it. I know it happened."

Mike looked at him. "They shot their prisoners."

Ubi looked up at him and met his gaze. "I know."

Mike reached for his drink. He was not given to anger, but there were moments when he felt it welling up within him. These people – the Germans – needed to have it brought home to them just what they had done. The country was full of people who said it was nothing to do with them – not a swastika in sight, not a party badge; a whole ghost country that had somehow disappeared when the Allies had arrived.

"I didn't want any of that to happen," said Ubi. "I don't expect you'll believe me, but I didn't."

Mike put down his drink. He felt immediately guilty. This was the man who had possibly saved his life. He reached out and placed a hand on Ubi's arm. "Of course I believe you. And I'm sorry – I'm tired. I've been flying too much, and it's tricky stuff. Coming in over the rooftops, missing the chimneys by inches. It takes it out of you."

Ubi nodded. "The people are very grateful," he said. "They can't quite believe that you're doing what you're doing, all for us. We were your enemies, and now you're doing this for us."

"War isn't the only thing," said Mike. "You get over it."

They raised their glasses to one another, repeating their first, tentative toast.

"So what now?" asked Mike.

Ubi explained about getting back to Ilse. "I'll wait. When it's possible again, I'll take my nephew back there."

Mike hesitated. "It might be possible," he said.

"What do you mean?"

"Did you hear about that man who did an involuntary trip? One of the loaders was shut in by mistake and had to take a cold ride back to Cologne."

Ubi said they had been warned to be careful. That man could have frozen to death.

"So if you and the boy," Mike continued, "were to stow away, we might not notice you until we had taken off and were well on our way. Do you see what I mean?"

Ubi looked about him. The habit of the last few years had become ingrained: circumspection, caution, silence.

Mike noticed, and smiled. "Look," he said. "You're free now. Nobody can harm you. That's all over."

Ubi looked at him with gratitude. It was so different for these Americans; they'd never had a government founded on hate. "When?" he asked.

Mike scratched his head. "Those repairs will be done by morning. We'll probably be off duty tomorrow, but we'll be flying in the next morning. Could you and your nephew be there?"

Ubi thought. Security at the gates was tight, but mostly for those going out. Theft had been a problem and the authorities were getting tougher.

"I could try," he said. "It could be hard to get Klaus in, but I'm friendly with one of the security men. He's German – we were at school together. He might be persuaded."

Mike reached into the bag he had with him – halfway between a briefcase and a rucksack. He took out a carton of cigarettes. "Would this help to smooth the way?"

"I think my friend smokes," said Ubi, smiling.

Klaus was wrapped in as many layers of clothing as they could manage, which made him look like the cocoon of some flying insect. The widow smothered him with kisses and urged Ubi to be careful. He thanked her and promised that he would send her money when he was able to do so. "I'm very grateful to you," he said. "I shan't forget."

He had reported in sick for the day. Arriving at the airport an hour or so before the time that Mike had given him, he saw that his friend was on duty, as they had planned it. Ubi had the papers to get in, and the friend explained to his superior that the child had an appointment to be seen by a doctor who was coming in on one of the flights. "I've seen the documents," he said. "And everything's in order."

The superior was busy with something else, and nodded his approval. They were in.

They waited in the unloading area. Ubi entertained the little boy with a toy he had brought with him – a small tin monkey on a string. He fed him pieces of chocolate and pointed out the stream of planes as they came in. The child watched wide-eyed, confused by the din of activity; at one point he wailed in fear, but was pacified by a particularly large piece of chocolate. Ubi watched the sky. It was a fine winter afternoon, with the sun painting the trees and buildings with gold. The aeroplanes appeared as specks of reflected light in the sky, grew larger and darker, and dropped down onto their perilous approach route through the buildings.

He knew the identifying number of Mike's aircraft, but he almost missed it as it did a balletic turn on the apron in preparation for unloading. But he saw it in time to follow the truck onto which his team would unload the cargo. He had already seen them and spoken to one or two of them.

"Why are you here?" his deputy asked. "You were meant to be sick."

"I have to look after this boy today," said Ubi. "I've brought him in to see the planes."

"You shouldn't."

"Well, I have."

He stood aside as the cargo of rice was unloaded. When the last sack had been dragged and manhandled into the truck, he approached the loading bay door and began to clamber into the plane. Hands reached out to help him; others took the child from him and spirited him into the storage area of the fuselage.

Mike said to him, "Everybody on board knows. They're okay. I told them what you did."

He was aware that he was being looked at with interest by two other men in flying gear. One of them made a thumbs-up sign; the other smiled.

"Sit down over there," said Mike. "Hold onto the boy."

They were not refuelling, and they had to take their place in the line of aircraft readied for departure. The pitch of the engines rose, and in his terror Klaus clung more tightly to Ubi, who hugged him and tried to reassure him with half-remembered nursery rhymes, the words of which were lost in the roar of the engines and the rattling of the aircraft's fuselage. *Hänschen klein / ging allein / in die weite Welt hinein . . . Sieben Jahr / trüb und klar / Hänschen in der Fremde war . . .*

Eventually the terrified child fell asleep, and was still sleeping when the plane dropped down one hundred and twenty miles later to make a bumpy landing on American asphalt in the western zone.

"Guess what?" said Mike to the control tower wireless operator. "I believe we have stowaways."

FOUR
MOTODROM

25

Ilse had prepared an attic bedroom for Klaus immediately above the room she occupied with Ubi. She had brightened up a counterpane by sewing onto it animal shapes cut from a bolt of red felt. She had been given the felt, a precious commodity, as a present and had been keeping it for some special purpose; this, she decided, was the moment to use it. There was an elephant, with trunk raised, a line of camels, and a bloated hippopotamus. She had not anticipated the small boy's reaction to the sight of the quilt, which had been one of fear, and a terrified seeking of refuge behind Ubi's legs.

Ubi sought to reassure her. "He'll get used to it," he said. "Remember what children in Berlin have seen."

She understood. She had been surprised by the resilience of children, when she knew what they had witnessed. There were gangs of them everywhere, it seemed, groups of semi-feral youngsters who survived among the city ruins, living from hand to mouth, emerging to steal whatever they could lay their hands on before slipping back into the shadows. Theft was their lifeline, although some of them, boys as well as girls, knew that more money could be made in prostitution and took advantage of the fact, beyond the reach of the authorities, their tired, world-weary faces reflecting their loss of childhood and the daily pain of their furtive, degraded lives.

At least Klaus had had a home and an adult to look after him. But now, having lost the security of the widow's flat in Berlin and the familiar routine of his life there, he was uncertain and confused. Ilse's advances to him were culinary, but the dishes she concocted herself, which included treats she was sure he would never have seen in Berlin, were often rebuffed without any explanation; questions addressed to him were rarely acknowledged, and he withdrew into a sullen and resentful private world.

"Grief," said a friend, a nurse, who had tried – and failed – to get through to him.

"And there's no cure for that," said Ilse.

The nurse shook her head. "Love," she said. "And patience." She added, as an afterthought, "Time."

Ilse knew her friend was right: she would give this child those three things and he would get better, just as Germany itself would recover from its nightmare. She could already see it happening around her; a factory had opened in their town and it was turning out furniture – functional items at first: beds and chests of drawers that were even being exported to France, people said – but that was just the beginning; there would soon be more expensive things. The inn itself was doing well; the British officers had moved on – they had their own buildings now – but Germans themselves were beginning to travel and look for places to stay. There was money again; not much, and there was a limit to what it could acquire, but the grinding poverty of those first few years was slowly being relieved. It showed in people's demeanour: the broken, almost dazed look of defeat was no longer universal. People were smiling again; wearily, cautiously perhaps, but smiling nonetheless.

Ilse and Ubi married. Their wedding was a quiet affair: there was no family to invite on Ubi's side, apart from two cousins in Hamburg, who for various reasons were unable to make the journey; Ilse's parents had recently divorced and were uncomfortable about attending together. It was simpler, she thought, for them to marry with the minimum of fuss, which is what they eventually did.

Ubi had acquired a motorcycle – a battered machine that he spent long evenings restoring. They used this for their honeymoon trip, three days of meandering through countryside so untouched by the war that it might never have happened. Klaus was looked after by one of the maids in the hotel who had become fond of him, and spoiled him with treats of marzipan animals she made from sugar and almonds acquired from her black-marketeer lover.

Klaus started to call Ilse *Mutti*. She cried the first time he did this, struggling to contain her sobs. Ubi asked her what was wrong, and she whispered her reply to him. He stroked her hand. They had been trying for a child of their own, with no success, and he feared it would never happen. She said to him, "I think that he loves me now," and he replied, "He does; of course he does."

Two years passed. Klaus began school, and showed an aptitude for anything requiring manual skills. His teacher praised him for his politeness, and rewarded him with gold stars on his exercise books. He was happy enough at school, although from time to time he was bullied because he looked different from the other children. He said one day, "Why is my hair like this? Will it change?"

Ilse said, "It's lovely hair, Klaus."

"They laugh at me."

"Who? Who laughs at you?"

"Some boys."

She wanted to find the perpetrators and shake them, but

Ubi persuaded her that Klaus would have to fight his own battles. "Things will change," he said. "Germany is going to be different. Nobody is going to torment anybody again."

Ubi finished the restoration of the *Motodrom*. He had as yet no plans for it, although he had taken to practising riding it – tentatively at first, making quick forays from the angled lower section to the vertical wall, before dropping back to the safety of the lower level. Then, emboldened, he completed his first full ride, soaring higher until he sped around just below the level of the raised viewing platform. Ilse and Klaus came to witness this, and shrieked with admiration as Ubi waved to them with one hand while steering with the other.

"One day," said Ubi, "we'll start this thing properly. We'll open it to the public."

Ilse smiled. "Perhaps."

"But we must," insisted Ubi. "What's the point of having a *Motodrom* if you don't use it?"

"Perhaps," she repeated.

Early in 1950, Ubi decided to write to Mike. They had not met again since Mike had flown him from Berlin; Ubi, though, had thought of his friend from time to time and had wondered whether he was still stationed in Germany. There was a certain embarrassment for him in contacting Mike – he felt that it could be seen as an attempt to ingratiate himself, which he was reluctant to do. People like Mike had every reason to dislike Germans, and he felt that he did not wish to press himself upon him. Yet he wanted him to know about Klaus, and how he had settled, and how their lives were getting better. He wanted to express gratitude for what Mike and his fellow Americans had done. The Russians had wanted to punish Germany, and had done so; their plan was to transform the country into one giant potato farm, people said, a feudal empire given over to the growing of food for Russia. America had been different; it was helping them back on their feet, and he wanted to say thank you, again, for that.

He addressed his letter to Mike at his base in Wiesbaden. In it, he told him what had happened since his return. He put in a picture of Klaus, standing beside Ilse, holding the small wooden figure of Pinocchio Mike had found abandoned in a Berlin ruin – a dead child's toy, he thought. Pinocchio's nose had been broken, and was half its original size, but the paint on his cheeks was still bright and rosy. He told Mike about the improving fortunes of the inn, and about the restoration of the *Motodrom*. He invited him to visit them if he ever had the chance to travel their way. He signed the letter, *Your grateful friend, Ubi.*

He received no reply. After a few weeks he wrote again, a shorter note this time, in which he asked whether his original letter had been delivered. This time there came a response – a brown envelope, on which his name and address were typed. Ilse handed it to him in the office at the inn.

"He's answered you now," she said. "Your first letter must have been lost."

Ubi opened the envelope. The letter within was typed, on paper that had a printed military heading. Glancing at the signature before he read it, he saw that it was not signed by Mike.

Dear Herr Dietrich, the letter began, *I am writing in reply to your recent letter addressed to Lieutenant Michael Rogers. I regret to inform you that Lieutenant Rogers lost his life in an aircraft accident in May 1949. This incident occurred in Berlin, during the airlift. I have forwarded your letter to his widow, who is now living in England.*

Ubi read the letter several times before passing it on to Ilse. He was mute. She read it and shook her head. "One more," she said.

He nodded, and reached out to take the paper back from her. "I feel very sad," he said.

"Of course you must," she said. "Perhaps you can write to his wife. This major . . ." She gestured to the letter. "You can write to this major and ask him to forward a letter to his wife."

"Yes," said Ubi. "I shall." He paused. "It would have been a landing accident, you know. It was so dangerous – all those planes circling above Berlin, round and round, and then having to drop down over the buildings. No wonder they crashed."

She was watching him. "Do you think there will come a time when we stop hurting one another?"

He was surprised by her question. "Hurting one other?"

"Yes. The Berlin blockade: what was that but an attempt by the Russians to hurt Berlin – to hurt all of us."

He sighed. "The Russians are full of anger. But then . . ." He sighed again.

She waited for him to continue.

"But then there is such a thing as righteous anger, don't you think?"

He was right, she thought.

He turned away. "But I wonder how long we are going to be punished? How long will we have to hang our heads in shame for what we did? All our lives, do you think? All our children's lives too?"

She shrugged. "Perhaps for all of our lives." The thought

seemed impossibly bleak – a life sentence. "I don't know. Unless they forgive us."

"They won't," he said. "The British will. The Americans and the French too. But not the Russians. I don't see them doing that, do you?"

He composed the letter to Val that evening. He had never met her, but Mike had told him a little bit about her during the conversation in the bar in Berlin. He had never written a letter of this nature before, and he decided to write it first in German and then ask Ilse to translate it into English for him. *I have been told the sad news of your husband's accident*, he began. *This causes me sorrow. Your husband was most kind to me. I shall remember him with great affection.* He showed it to Ilse, who said that it was perfect. "The English do not like to make a big fuss," she said. "They are very reserved. Such a letter will be a great comfort to an English person."

26

The air force was generous. As the widow of an officer killed in action, Val was entitled to a pension. She could go to the United States if she wished and would be assisted in finding accommodation and employment. She could go wherever she wanted to go, and efforts would be made to help her find her feet wherever she chose to settle.

Mike's family said that she was welcome to come to Indiana, where his grandparents would take her in and provide a home for Tommy. It would be on their farm, they said, but there was an elementary school quite close and Tommy could go there. Muncie was ten miles away and she might get a job in the town if she wanted one. They knew somebody in a local bank who could get her a job as a trainee book-keeper. You would never want for work if you were a book-keeper, they said.

It was not an easy decision. She was missing Mike with an intensity that she had never thought possible. It was a feeling of emptiness, a dull ache, constantly present, impossible to subdue by any of the nostrums that people suggested – busying yourself, consciously thinking of other things, counting your blessings, and so on. None of this worked. In her view, their short marriage had been perfect; not once had she felt any irritation or anger; not once had the thought crossed her mind that this partnership between two people of such different backgrounds could turn out to be ill-starred. She had begun to be American, talking of Indiana as home, conversing with the other air force wives on their terms, wearing what they liked to wear, laughing at the same things, becoming a member of what seemed to be a large club of infinite possibilities. But now all that had turned to dust because her rationale for being like this had disappeared. The new person she had become was all to do with Mike, and now that he had gone, the new identity had gone too.

She wrote to Mike's family to thank them for their kindness, but explained that she would return to her aunt's house. It would be easier to care for Tommy there, she said, although she did not say why this should be so. Their reply was one of disbelief. How could it be easier to care for a child in England, where there were still shortages and money was tight? Did she not think that she owed it to her son to bring him up in a place where there were opportunities? She could have written back to ask *What do you know of England?* But she did not do so; she realised that Mike's grandparents simply wanted to have their grandson's little boy, and that was something that he would have understood. She wrote back a conciliatory letter. Yes, she understood all the points they raised; yes, Tommy would have many opportunities in America, but she still felt on balance it would be better for him if she were happy too, and she had never been to America and could not be sure that she would be happy there. What if she did not like it? What if she felt lonely and cut off from her family back in England?

She went home earlier than she had planned. The air force had been prepared for her to stay in the officers' accommodation on the base, but she thanked them and said that this would not be necessary. She left everything behind – virtually all the possessions they had accumulated together, taking only photographs and clothing; she was ending a chapter and she did not wish to be cluttered with things of the past.

After a day or two at home it was as if she had never been away. Annie was still running the post office, her room was as she had left it, and there were even clothes in her wardrobe that still fitted her. Annie had installed a cot at the end of Val's bed; this was for Tommy, although he was now of an age to sleep in something larger. She had also bought him several new sets of clothes, although these were already too small for him; Mike had been tall, and Tommy was taking after him.

One thing was different: Willy had moved into Archie's farmhouse, where he occupied the spare room at the back of the house. Archie's arthritis had become worse, and he now spent most of the day immobile in the kitchen, following what was happening on the farm with an old pair of army field binoculars. He did not need to watch too closely; Willy had taken the farm in hand, had clipped the hedgerows and cropped the patches of rank grazing land. New fruit trees had been planted, and new silos built. He had even managed to find the wire for new fences and had put these up himself, while repairing some of the older sections of fencing that went back fifty or sixty years.

At first, Willy was shy. Tommy had forgotten him, of course, and Willy, puzzled by his reticence, kept his distance. But that soon changed, and it was not long before he was showing the boy around the farm and teaching him to look for eggs in the hen coop.

"He loves being with you, Willy," said Val. "He talks about you non-stop, you know."

Willy beamed with pleasure. "He has the makings of a farmer," he said. "It shows."

Val smiled, but she had her reservations. When would

Tommy realise that Willy had his limitations? And might not somebody like Willy hold back a child? She reflected, with regret, on the sort of father Mike had been, and on the fact that Tommy would probably have no recollection of him in later life. She would try, of course, to keep his memory alive, but it would mean little to a child of Tommy's age.

Tommy started at the village school. Now that he was out of the house for the entire morning, Val looked for a job. A new medical practice had opened up in the town a few miles away and they needed a receptionist. Val applied and was appointed. She enjoyed the responsibility and the variety that the work provided, and it meant, too, that she met people.

Annie asked her if she would remarry, and she shook her head. "Not for a long time," she said.

"I can understand that," said Annie. "But the heart gets better, you know. Give it the chance, and it'll get better."

Val laughed. "Who'll want me? A man doesn't like to take on a woman with another man's child. Men steer clear of that sort of thing."

Annie disagreed. "Any man who gets you will be very fortunate," she said.

Then Willy proposed. Archie had unwittingly put the idea in his head. He had disclosed that he would be moving to a stockman's cottage that had been lying empty on the farm, and Willy could have the main farmhouse, if he wished; he was used to it now and it was easy to run the farm from there.

Willy said to Val, "Archie's given me the house. He says I can live there by myself."

"That's kind of him, Willy," said Val. "And you're good to him – anybody can see that."

Willy brushed the compliment aside. "It's a big place," he said. 'Too big for one person."

"Then get somebody to share it with you," said Val. "There's that tractor man down at Dunbar's place who's looking for somewhere. He might—"

Willy did not let her finish. "Or you," he said.

Val stared at him. "Me? But I live with Auntie – here – at the post office."

Willy reached out to take her hand. His skin felt rough. Val laughed nervously. "I could come to visit you," she said.

"That's not what I meant," said Willy. "You and I . . . well, we could get fixed up together."

She caught her breath. "I don't think so, Willy. It's very kind of you, of course, but . . ."

"Because I love you," said Willy. "I've always loved you – right from the beginning."

He spoke with such disarming frankness that her heart gave a leap. "That's kind. Thank you, Willy."

"No, I mean it." He paused, looking askance at her.   "You don't think I'm stupid, do you?"

She assured him that she did not.

"Because all I want to do is to look after you," he said. "And Tommy."

She knew that what he said was true: that was what he wanted. And then she thought about her own feelings, and how she was sure that she would never stop loving Mike, and that if she were to accept Willy's proposal she could still do that; she had always thought it possible to love more than one person at the same time, and there were, after all, different types of love, as people learned in wartime, when, in the knowledge of the fragility of any human plans, they made do, took what they could get, learned to patch things together. She was tired. If she married Willy she would have a place to live and there would be somebody who loved Tommy to look after both of them. The world was an uncertain place, full of disappointment. She wanted to protect Tommy from that, whatever should happen to her. "If I marry you," she said to Willy, "will you let me . . ." She hesitated, searching for the right way of expressing what she had in mind. "Will you let me decide what to do?" No, that was not quite right. "You see," she went on, "I want to play my full part . . ."

He smiled. "But of course you can do that. I don't mind."

Annie received the news in silence. Then, trying hard to conceal her surprise, she said, "It'll be good for Tommy."

"Yes," said Val. "It will."

Annie gave her a searching look. "Is that why you're doing it?"

Val bit her lip. "He's a good man."

"I know that," said Annie. "But . . ."

"There are different ways of being happy," said Val.

Annie nodded. "You're a good girl, Val Eliot," she said.

Val was embarrassed by the compliment. But there was something else. "And Archie has told him that he can take over the farm," she said. "He'll let to him for a very small rent, and then he says he'll come into it eventually – when Archie goes."

Annie raised an eyebrow. "That's a generous gift."

"Archie has no family."

"No," said Annie. "Nor does he. But now he does, you see."

27

In 1951, Ilse received an invitation to a wedding in a village in Oxfordshire. One of the British majors, the one who had taught Ubi English, had left the army and taken a job as a teacher in a boys' boarding school. He was marrying the daughter of the local doctor and had sent an invitation to Ilse, with whom he had maintained a correspondence since leaving Germany. Ubi had also been invited, but was unable to make the journey as somebody had to stay behind to look after the hotel. He was uncomfortable, too, about going to England. "They might not want to see us . . . just yet," he said.

Ilse laughed at him. "But they've invited us," she pointed out.

"I don't mean them – the major. I don't mean him. I mean people in general. What if we turned a corner, and there was Winston Churchill?"

This brought more laughter. "Mr Churchill would be very polite. I'm sure he would say *guten Tag*."

It was not a journey undertaken lightly. In Germany things were returning to normal, step by cautious step; in England the Festival of Britain, an ambitious official effort to persuade people to address the future with optimism, was under way, but people still felt bruised by years of privation. Travel was still a luxury for both nations.

Ilse bought a new dress for the wedding and made the journey by train to Calais, where she boarded the ferry to Dover. The following day she arrived at her small hotel in the village where the wedding was due to take place. At the wedding, although the major and his bride were polite and welcoming, the other guests seemed stand-offish. She sensed that she was being pointed out as the German guest – the subject of whispers and sideways glances.

She had a day in hand after the wedding before she had to get back to Dover for her return ferry. She had with her the diary in which she had written Val's address, and she asked the woman who kept the hotel whether it would be possible to get there and back in a day. She and Val had exchanged letters since that first letter of sympathy, writing to one another every two or three months, as pen friends. Val had said that if Ilse ever came to England she should come to see her, and Ilse had reciprocated. Neither had imagined that either would ever take up the invitation, but now Ilse found herself feeling a certain curiosity about her unmet friend.

The hotel-keeper told her that it would not be a complicated trip. There was a bus that stopped at the edge of the village; this would take her all the way to a town near Val's village. She could go from there by taxi.

She sent a telegram to warn Val of her arrival, not knowing whether it would reach her in time. She arrived at the post office, to which she had addressed her letters to Val. Annie greeted her warmly; the telegram had been received a few hours earlier. "I know all about you," she said. "I'll telephone Val and tell her you're here."

Val collected her in the farm van and took her back to meet Willy and Tommy. The two women's conversation was stilted at first, but after a while it became more relaxed.

"Our husbands had a very good friendship," said Ilse.

Val sighed. 'War is unnatural – friendship isn't."

"Yes," said Ilse. "We women know that."

Val thought: we had to fight, though, and it was because of you. But she stopped herself, because she knew that forgiveness demanded that such thoughts be put to one side.

Ilse caught her bus back to her hotel late that afternoon. She felt herself becoming emotional when she said goodbye to Val and to Tommy.

"You will continue to write, won't you?" she asked Val as they stood at the bus stop.

"Of course," promised Val. "It will be much easier now that you have seen the farm and we've met. Much easier."

The bus took Ilse off, its tired engine spluttering as it drew away from the stop. She waved to Val and Tommy through the window beside her seat. The window was dirty, and somebody had traced a message on its surface: *Harry loves Geraldine: true.* She raised a finger and wrote underneath it, *I have a true friend.* It was an odd, childish thing to do. Harry, who had written the other message, was probably sixteen or seventeen – unless, of course, it was Geraldine who had written those words, in the hope that what she said was true was really the truth.

Everything changed. A great wave of prosperity washed over Germany as the pinched, hungry years of the fifties gave way to a decade of plenty. In Britain, crisis followed crisis, as the world folded in over a country that was exhausted to its very bones. The youthful vanquished rebuilt and prospered; the aged victors looked on in puzzlement as their lucrative empire crumbled. Ilse sold the inn to a wealthy businessman who wanted it for a brother-in-law who had managed to escape from the East. Ubi moved the *Motodrom* to a site in the countryside. There was a house attached to the field in which the *Motodrom* now stood, and that became their home. A young mechanic, an enthusiastic motorcyclist, was taken on as the principal rider, and he brought with him a friend who joined him on the wall. A new road had been built nearby, an arterial highway that brought a stream of visitors to the attraction.

Ubi said to Ilse, "Did you ever imagine this? Ever?"

They were sitting outside the *Motodrom*; inside, the roar of motorcycles and the rattle of the wooden planks that made up the wall reached a climax. The cheers of the crowd became raucous applause.

"They're enjoying it," said Ilse. And then, "I would never have believed we would be doing this. Running a *Motodrom*?"

"Yes. And everything else. The war. Klaus. Us." He smiled at her and touched her hand gently. "Very few people imagine their own future accurately. And then they're often pleasantly surprised."

Ubi occasionally rode the *Motodrom* himself, but he knew that Ilse did not like it, and he was careful in the routines he performed. The two young men had no such scruples and shot up and down, their paths intersecting with a bravado that made the spectators gasp with pleasure.

'If you kill yourselves," Ilse warned them, "you'll have only yourselves to blame."

"No we won't," said the younger of the two. "We won't be around to blame anybody."

"Don't tempt providence," Ilse retorted.

Ubi taught Ilse how to ride a motorcycle – not on the *Motodrom*, but sedately on the roads. She enjoyed this, and he bought her a modest machine of her own. He acquired for himself a large Ducati, painted red, and with gleaming chrome. They rode away together at weekends, leaving Klaus with Ilse's aunt and putting the young men in charge of the *Motodrom*. They rode down to Munich and to Regensburg. They joined a motorcycle club; Ubi became president while Ilse was elected treasurer. Klaus watched. He said, "I'm going to get a motorcycle too one day."

"One day," said Ubi, non-committally.

A month later, Ilse wrote to Val: *How do you stop a boy doing dangerous things? One of the young men who works on our* Motodrom *has somehow got hold of a miniature motorcycle and I caught him putting Klaus on it.*

You can't stop them, came the reply. *Boys do foolish things. It's what they do.*

Things went well for Val and Willy too. They had moved from the post office to live on the farm, and Willy had helped Archie get the stockman's cottage into order. They had installed a bath and a new range in the farmhouse kitchen, and she had sewn new curtains from material that Annie had obtained from somewhere. Annie was always getting hold of material, somehow or other – it had become a bit of a family joke. On good days, Archie would come up from his cottage and sit with her in the kitchen – where it was warmest – to look out on the fields that he could no longer work in, because of his arthritis. He knew every inch of the land, she thought, every inch. He would have cared for it, year after year, and his father would have done exactly the same, without complaint, without questioning their destiny to nurture this little bit of England for their lifetime, and then hand it over to the next generation to do the same.

Tommy would not do that, though, and they would have to find somebody else to run the farm in due course. Val knew, even when he was still a small boy, that he would do something different; that he would be an engineer. He was fascinated by machinery and how things worked. When he was seven, she bought him a book called *The Boy's Book of How Everything Works*, which contained cutaway illustrations of the insides of ships and locomotives and even planes. It was all laid out there, in coloured diagrams, and he had pored over these, often with Willy, discussing the mechanisms that made these things work. Willy was learning every bit as much as Tommy was, she felt; she overheard a conversation about jet propulsion.

"Where does the air go, Tommy?"

Tommy had taken Willy's finger and moved it to a place on the drawing. "It goes in there. You see? There. And then it gets heated up and it comes out there with a whoosh."

"Which makes the plane go forward?"

"Yes, Willy. Forward, you see."

She smiled at the memory. It did not matter to Tommy that Willy was slow to take new things in; the boy seemed to take that in his stride, and even took pleasure in explaining something that Willy was not immediately grasping. And later, when Tommy was old enough to understand, she explained to him about how Willy had agreed to look after them and how he worked hard to make up for the fact that they had lost his real father.

"He flew an aeroplane," she said. "Your first dad. He was a pilot."

"In the war?"

"Yes, in the war, as I've told you, lots of times – remember?"

"He was American?'

She nodded. "Yes, he was American, Tommy. He came from a place called Muncie, Indiana. He used to tell me about it."

"But you never went there?"

She took a moment to answer. That was an unfulfilled promise in a way – to Mike. Perhaps she would honour it some day, and she would take Tommy and show him the place where his father came from. "No, I didn't go there myself. But maybe one day you and I . . ."

"Yes. Yes. Please."

"We'll try."

She took a deep breath. She could so easily cry, but children became very anxious if an adult cried without reason – or without a reason they could comprehend. "There's another thing about your first dad – he was a very brave man. Some day you'll understand just how brave he was, but for now just believe me – he was a brave man."

He was watching her.

"And here's yet another thing," she said. "We had a dog, you know. We had a dog with a funny name."

"How funny?"

"He was called Peter Woodhouse. And you know what? He sometimes went off with your dad in his plane. He was what they call a mascot."

"What's that?"

"It's an animal that people sometimes have to keep them company – they sometimes think that a mascot brings good luck." She paused. "Which I think might just be true."

He looked unconvinced. "How can an animal bring you good luck?"

She shrugged. "I don't quite know. But they do, I think. They can help when you're in danger. That's what those pilots thought."

"My dad thought that?"

"I think he probably did."

The boy looked thoughtful. "Do animals go to heaven when they die? Like people?"

One could answer from one's head, she thought, or from one's heart.

"I don't know," she replied. She touched him lightly on his head; on the sandy-coloured hair that came from his father. "But perhaps . . . just perhaps, they do. Perhaps dogs, for instance, go to a special heaven for dogs."

"With lots of bones for them to chew?"

She laughed. "Yes, with lots of bones, and plenty of smells. Dogs would love that, don't you think? Plenty of smells for them to sniff at."

"And rabbits to chase?"

"Yes, lots of rabbits. The rabbits that had been bad on earth, maybe – they'd be sent to dog heaven, which wouldn't be so much fun for them. The good rabbits would go to a place where *they* chased the dogs."

"Was Peter Woodhouse a good dog?"

"A very good dog."

"So he'll be in dog heaven?"

She smiled. "Yes, I expect he will be. Doing his job – which is to watch over us, I think. You and me. He'll be watching."

FIVE

AFTERWARDS

28

In June 1981, in the southern German city of Regensburg, a meeting took place in the office of a quietly spoken lawyer. The lawyer, Franz Huber, was careful, almost fussy, in his manner; this suited his practice, which was mostly concerned with domestic affairs – family property, wills, and the like – and with the day-to-day issues of small businesses. He had a talent for persuading clients to adopt what he described as the "wise and cautious solution" to the complexities of their affairs. He was fond of saying "Nobody has ever regretted erring on the side of caution" – an observation that, under any scrutiny, would soon be shown to be false, but Herr Huber had little interest in missed opportunities.

"Frau Dietrich," he said, tapping his pencil discreetly on the edge of his desk. "This English lady? May I ask: have you known her for a long time?"

On the other side of his desk, Ilse tried to conceal her irritation. She had never liked Herr Huber, even if Ubi had thought highly of him. They had had few professional dealings – there was not much call for that – but Ubi knew him from the swimming club they had both been members of, and had mentioned him from time to time. She knew that Ubi had placed his affairs in Herr Huber's hands, and she knew that this would mean she would have to deal with him in due course.

"Many years," she replied.

"And your husband knew her too?"

She nodded. "It was through him that we met, you see – a long time ago. My husband knew her husband, and that was how I knew about her. It was one of those strange things that happened in those days. People were brought together in odd ways."

He raised an eyebrow. "I don't wish to pry," he said. "But here you are, proposing to give your two employees a half share in the business, while you and this English lady go off on this trip you've been talking about . . ."

She kept her temper. There was no point in antagonising the man. "She has a name, Herr Huber. Mrs Rogers. I call her Val. The English are less formal than we are, as I'm sure you're aware."

"Yes, of course. Mrs Rogers. Forgive me. Well, I really want to make sure that this Mrs Rogers isn't persuading you to take this step. The late Herr Dietrich – your husband, of course – would not have wished you to divest yourself at this stage of the business he had built up. She is a newcomer, so to speak . . ."

She shook her head. "She is not a newcomer, Herr Huber. She has been coming to see me for years now. And we're only going away for a couple of months." And there was more. "These two employees have been with me for six years now. They have been very loyal."

The pace of the pencil-tapping increased – until he noticed that her eyes were fixed on it, and he rapidly put it away.

"You're going off on your motorcycles," he muttered.

"On one motorcycle," she corrected him. "I have a great deal of experience with motorcycles, as you can imagine. Herr Dietrich and I used to go on our holidays that way. We rode all the way down to Italy. A large motorcycle is very comfortable for the pillion passenger – just as it is for the driver."

She saw a thin smile play about his lips. She did not have to justify herself to him, she thought. "The important thing is to be happy." Who had said that? Oh, hundreds of people, she thought; hundreds and hundreds of people through the ages, and all of them right. Because it was the important thing – the most important thing of all, when you came to think about it.

She glanced out of the window. There was a large tree directly outside, and its branches were moving in the breeze. In the distance, a hillside rose up to meet the pale summer sky. Perhaps it would be best to explain to him what had happened; this dry, essentially humourless lawyer might just understand – if she explained the history.

"My husband served in the war," she said.

She held his gaze. There was a flicker; just a flicker.

"And in the course of his service, he met an American airman."

His face was immobile. *He doesn't wish to be reminded.*

He spoke. "I see. An American airman."

"Yes. And then they met later on – during the Berlin Airlift."

Herr Huber relaxed. That was a different narrative, with a different set of victims.

"The American was married to an Englishwoman. He met her when he was stationed in England during the war. She came with him when he was based here in Germany – they were down in Wiesbaden, although he had to fly all over. He was one of the pilots who went into Berlin."

He was comfortable now. "That was so very important," he said. "If they hadn't done that . . ." He shrugged. "The Soviets would have taken everything eventually. I doubt if we would be here today, having this conversation. We have a lot to thank the Americans for."

Ilse said, "You are right. It was very important. And they were brave men."

"Of course they were."

"He was one of the ones who was killed," she continued. "It was towards the end of the blockade – just days before, I think. They had to fly in all sorts of conditions. I don't think it was anybody's fault. Something went wrong, and his plane went down. We were in touch with his widow afterwards."

"Wartime friendships," said Herr Huber. "They can be very strong, I think."

"His widow went back to England – to her people."

Herr Huber nodded. "It's always best," he said. "If you can go home, that's the best thing to do. Always." He paused. "And then?"

"I wrote to her – my husband, you see, was not a very good correspondent. Men aren't, you see, and wives have to . . ." She trailed away. He was looking reproachful.

"*Some* men, Frau Dietrich. "*Some* men – not all of them."

She inclined her head. "Yes, you're right – not all men. But, as I was saying, we wrote to one another over the years. Every year there was a Christmas card – that sort of thing – and a letter as well. She married again. She lived on a farm, over there; I went to see her, and then she came over to Germany every other year to stay with us."

The lawyer inclined his head. 'I understand, Frau Dietrich – and it is not for me to interfere in your plans."

"No," she said. "It is not."

Dust, white dust of the sort that for its fineness took time to settle, was thrown up in a small cloud behind them as Ilse applied the brakes of the motorbike. It was hot, and when she switched off the engine the air was filled with the screech of cicadas. Someone in the distance was cutting wood with a buzz-saw, the old branches of a vine perhaps, because there were vineyards stretched out across the slopes of the hillsides here.

She silently coasted the heavy bike into the shade thrown by a sculpted birch tree. These trees formed a regimented line along the edge of the village; below them the land fell away sharply to the plains below. On the other side of the road was the village, a cluster of buildings ascending to a tangle of woods above which the sky, pale in this heat, was dizzying in its emptiness.

The village had no proper piazza, the public space being the area in front of the shops and houses that made up the main street. At the end of this one-sided street was a church, its open door looking to all intents and purposes like the mouth of a cave. At least it would be cool in there, with the rock as its floor and the shelter it provided from the relentless sun.

They stretched when they dismounted, taking off their helmets and putting them on the seats of the motorcycle before they stretched their legs. They had been riding non-stop since Florence that morning; the day before they had ridden all the way from Milan and both had felt the aches that came with such a long spell on the road.

Now, though, there was lunch to look forward to, and the village at least boasted a proper restaurant with umbrellas outside and a table of old men sitting smoking and nursing glasses of the local red wine.

They sat at one of the other tables outside. There was a greeting from the table of locals, who had smiled at the sight of two women on a motorbike, and smiled even more when they saw their age. This would be talked about for days, analysed and speculated upon in a village where nothing ever happened other than the arrival of passers-by.

The proprietor brought them a large bottle of carbonated water. They sipped on this while they scrutinised the menu, which offered what it described as the "particular delights of the region".

Ilse said, "Well, I feel we're really on our way now. Home seems a long way away."

"It does," said Val. "And it is."

"With all its cares."

"Yes, with all its cares. Your wall of death . . . It's in good hands, isn't it?"

"Those two young men are completely reliable," said Ilse. "They're never happier than when they're going round and round, making the girls scream with delight. All our young men have been the same."

Val laughed. "What girl wouldn't like to see a young man going round and round a wall of death?" She paused. "Did you ever go on it yourself?"

Ilse nodded. "I used to – now and then. I rode one of the smaller bikes. I sometimes went on when Ubi was riding. He enjoyed it. He was never really happy running the inn, but when we gave that up to concentrate on the *Motodrom* he was very happy."

Val lifted her glass of water to her mouth. The bubbles were sharp on the tongue; tiny needles of sensation. "You must miss him," she said.

Ilse looked back at her. "Yes, just as you must miss Mike."

"When you marry again," said Val, "you don't talk about that too much. You're meant to be over it, but you aren't, you know. Not really."

"We have our boys, of course."

"Yes," said Val. "And Tommy's a good son. Now that he's working in London I don't see so much of him – and he's got his own young family now. Your Klaus – do you see a lot of him?"

"It's not too far to Stuttgart," said Ilse. "Three hours or so. He's doing well. He's never liked motorbikes since he fell off one when he was just a boy. He loves cars – which is why he's working for those people in Stuttgart – but motorbikes, no. He disapproves of my riding, you realise?"

Val smiled. "I think it shows we brought them up right if they disapprove of our behaviour."

"Perhaps. No, you're right. You're right."

The proprietor came to take their order. "You've ridden down here all the way from Germany?" he asked.

"We have," answered Ilse. "And we're going on to Naples. Then Sicily. Palermo."

The proprietor suppressed a smile.

"You could join us if you like," said Val. "Do you have a motorbike?'

The proprietor laughed. "I have a wife," he said.

Ilse made a gesture of disappointment. "Oh well."

They were brought their food.

Afterwards, with coffee on the table, they sat under the shade of the umbrella and looked down onto the plains.

"You know," said Val, "there was something I was told that I don't think I ever passed on to you."

"Oh?"

"Yes. Mike told me. He said that when they were in Holland – when they were hiding from . . ." She stopped herself.

"From the Germans," Ilse supplied.

"Yes. But it was a long time ago. Let's say, different Germans."

"Something happened?"

"Yes. They had a dog with them."

"I heard about that," said Ilse.

"And your husband, your Ubi, was ordered to shoot the dog."

Ilse winced.

"But he did not," continued Val. "He saved the dog's life by firing a shot in the air."

Ilse was silent. "He did that?" she asked at last.

"Yes," said Val.

Ilse looked down at the tablecloth. "I'm glad you told me that," she said. "I'm very glad."

"You never knew it?"

"No. But I'm grateful you told me, because it makes me proud of him."

They were both silent. Then Ilse said, "Do you think it's possible to love somebody who isn't there any longer? To carry on loving him?"

Val looked up at the sky. A hint of a cooling breeze had sprung up and it touched her now. Swallows dipped and swooped in pursuit of prey in the higher layers of air; tiny dots of pirouetting black. The question was not a casual one, she thought; this was as important as anything they had said to one another. "Of course it is," she said. "Of course."

"Are you sure?"

"Yes, I'm quite sure." And then she added, "Look up there; look at the birds."

"What about them?"

"Nothing."

She thought: *You can go on loving people a long time after they have left you; you can love them every bit as much as you loved them when they were still here. Love lasts. Love grows stronger. Love lasts a lifetime, and beyond.*